FUNERALS FOR HORSES

FUNERALS FOR HORSES

BY CATHERINE RYAN HYDE

RUSSIAN HILL PRESS
SAN FRANCISCO

Russian Hill Press, San Francisco
www.russianhill.com
© 1997 by Catherine Ryan Hyde
All rights reserved. Published 1997
Printed in the United States of America
00 99 98 97 5 4 3 2 1

Book and jacket design by Kirk Franklin
This book is set in Minion

Library of Congress Cataloging-in-Publication Data
Hyde, Catherine Ryan.
 Funerals for Horses / by Catherine Ryan Hyde
     -1st ed.
[97-065291]
CIP
ISBN 0-9653524-3-9

THE GOD OF GROWING UP

MY BROTHER SIMON was forty-two years old. I pray he still is. I shame and cajole his family into believing with me, but their wicks have burned down, their flames left to flicker, like the light they pretend to leave on in the window for Simon, like their own dwindling lives.

He has been gone two months and four days.

I pray that somehow, somewhere, in presence or absence of pain and fear, he will turn forty-three tomorrow. But it's hard to reconcile myself to prayer.

As a young girl I decided, in light of prevailing evidence, that a child does not fall under god's jurisdiction until age eighteen. No one taught me this theory. It was my own carefully researched conclusion. After all, you can't vote, or fight a war, until that age, and to assume god washes his hands of our affairs until then settled a number of otherwise troubling questions.

In need of a sort of interim god, I adopted Simon, and forgot or similarly refused to switch over, until long past eighteen, until age thirty-six, until the calls came. First from Sarah, his wife, asking if I'd seen him, as he does tend to take off on short notice to visit me. Then the call three days later. They'd found his clothes, all of them. His suit, complete with checkbook, vest, shoes, tie, the whole nine yards. All strewn around a wooded area just below a freight line track in Central California. His jockey shorts and wallet were never found.

Until then I held my life together carefully, if not seamlessly, maintaining a greater degree of sanity than seems my birthright. This is Simon's doing, and none of my own.

Now, who knows?

Now even Raphael seems concerned about me, and, as Raphael is preparing to die of AIDS, as are all my lovers, his concern troubles me.

If not for other reasons, the deal is that I am to be concerned about him—them—and I dislike role reversals even more than other types of change. It forms a basis of excuse for me to shut Raphael out of my life, if a bit gradually, though we all knew I would when the sickness set in. I never promise them otherwise. I never pretend.

I stay awake until midnight. Now it is Simon's birthday. Now I have held still too long.

I write a note to my employer, who refused me a leave of absence, though not in so many words. He recited a speech suggesting that a hallmark of maturity is the strength to function in crisis.

I had listened carefully, then continued as if I hadn't heard, a purposeful validation of his assumptions about me. I am not as unstable as people tend to think, but I allow them their margin for error because it allows me mine.

Now I write seven notes, one to each of my lovers, to use a loosely applicable term. I have never had what one what might call a run-of-the-mill sexual encounter with any one of them, due to their exposure to the virus. But sex is what you make it, and we have always made do. To assume sex must take place within touching distance seems, to me, limited thinking.

I slip the notes into envelopes and label each with a name. Raphael. David. Mark. Carey. Ed. Jonathan. Jamey.

Raphael will find them first, I've no doubt, and he might be surprised. Each knows he is not the only one, but perhaps not that he is one of seven. Not that it matters now. This is not promiscuity on my part, not at its roots; more that so few women will make concessions to the HIV-positive male that I am forced to do far more than my share.

Raphael will come by in the morning, I think, and I will be gone. Now that he wears blotches on his forearms, and the rasp clings from his last bout with PCC pneumonia, he diligently insinuates himself into my life. It is a breach of agreement, albeit a silent agreement, and I suppose he feels he must force me to draw his line. He will not bow out with grace as others have done in the past. He will continue to knock, wearing his splotches offset against black jeans and shirt, dark circles, dark haze of beard, dark hair falling into his eyes. Even debilitated, Raphael maintains a Bohemian grace, an odd handsomeness.

His visits will continue until I refuse him or until I am gone, which is to say, there will be one more visit, to no avail. No, I am not hardhearted. I will miss Raphael. More than any of them.

Reverently, I dismantle the shrine-like arrangement of my brother Simon's photos, a forty-year-old blond child in a business suit.

I picture Raphael watching over my shoulder. If he were here, he'd say, *a healthy move, Ella.*

I would not tell him I only disturbed the photos because I'll need them with me on the road, both for solace and as exhibit A.

As I pack, he would say, *you'll never find him.*

I would scream at him for that. I would forbid him to ever say I cannot find Simon. I hear the screaming in my head. It sounds like my sister DeeDee, telling me I must never again suggest that Andy is not a real horse. Her hands locked around my throat when she screamed this in real life. I still miss DeeDee.

I am glad Raphael is not here.

In the morning I stick the notes on my door with push pins, a different color for each sweet, doomed man, whichever color I feel suits him best.

I clean out my bank accounts on the way out of town.

THEN:

I WAS BORN with the caul. According to Grandma Ginsberg, this signified great things. But it proved a disappointment. Yes, I was the smartest child in all of my classes, the most morbidly mature that any of my teachers had seen, save my sister DeeDee. Yes, I was spiritually advanced, but in my family this was nothing special.

I owe any additional senses, I believe, not to the caul but to the genes of my father, Gabriel Ginsberg, a man with an intimidating I.Q.

We only lived together as a family until I was four, but I hold vivid early memories. Mostly I remember my mother rousing us out of bed in the middle of the night, bundling us in blankets and packing us down to the police station to post my father's bail. This same scene played out on at least a half dozen separate occasions.

He always looked contrite, though still in good humor. He would try to kiss my mother on the cheek, but she would pull away.

She adored the man, needed him, and always assured the police she would keep him on a tighter leash. This was the only time their roles shifted, the only time he needed her, which I now suspect is why she never shortened his leash.

At the trials my mother pleaded with the judge not to jail him, claiming the family would starve. Despite the recurring nature of his offenses, the judge would always let him off with a fine, though a higher fine each time, and threaten prison the next time my father appeared before his bench.

I know all this because, although Simon was in school, my mother would pack DeeDee and me to court for lack of a babysitter. Grandma Ginsberg claimed failing health, especially in the wake of one of my father's arrests. I overheard her tell my mother that it didn't matter anyway, because we were entirely too young to understand a term like indecent exposure. She didn't realize that children file away such words, awaiting definition.

I'd sit enthralled on the car ride home, loving the back of my father's head. The thinning hair on top created a wild effect that no amount of Brylcreem could tame. It seemed to match the rest of the man: big, rangy, loosely strung and indistinct.

Until my father left, he took us every Sunday to visit Grandma Ginsberg, the one who put such stock in my caul.

She always watched *Picka Polka* on Sundays. I was keenly aware of missing *Deputy Dawg,* but had no authority to change channels.

Grandma Ginsberg pinched cheeks.

If there is something good I can say for the woman, and no doubt I am scratching, it's that she loved her family. Still, it was a draining, disturbing sort of love, a leeching of our life force. I tried to stand away as much as possible, which prompted the often-repeated invitation to shame, "You don't love your old grandma."

Once, my father chastised me in the car on the way home because he said I didn't act like I wanted to be there. I didn't want to be there. Nobody had warned me that I was supposed to act.

When my father left home, Grandma Ginsberg went down and never got up. She broke her hip within twenty-four hours of the news. My mother bundled us into the car and met the ambulance at City General, where I listened to Grandma's keening shrieks of pain and her self-aggrandizement, and stared at her translucent gray face in wide-eyed silence.

She came to our house to recover, but apparently recovery was not in her plans. She refused wheelchair, walker, crutches. She refused to sit up again. She refused even to lift her huge, uncooperative body onto her own bedpan, forcing my mother to lift her, to feed her, to administer her pills, to listen to her *kvetching*, to jump out of sleep to calm her unreasonable fears.

This my mother would do for the kin of a man who abandoned her. Much as I loathed Grandma Ginsberg, I used to openly hope for her longevity, assuming that my mother would die without the constant, unyielding torment.

Grandma Ginsberg lived in a dank, smelly back bedroom which children avoided as if by precognition, even neighbor children who didn't know her.

Later, after the sports sections began stacking up, we never invited neighbor children anyway.

When my father left, my mother began to pull the sports section out of the evening paper before bundling the leftovers for the Boy Scout paper drive. Nobody dared ask why until almost two years later, when the papers had been assigned their own closet, then spilled beyond it.

Simon had the guts, not me. Brave, honest Simon, twelve years old to my six, asked if he could throw them away.

"Certainly not," she said. "Your father will be home any day now, and the first thing he'll want is dinner and his sports section."

She swirled out of the room as if in a hurry, leaving me alone with my brother Simon, who twisted a finger around near his head as a comment on her mental acuity. I was shocked and impressed. How can a child admit a parent is unstable? To me it seemed equivalent to suggesting that the ground won't hold us up, or gravity won't stick us down to it. But Simon worked off a different set of laws. Simon stepped on cracks. Simon was never afraid to see.

I often thought it was Simon, not me, who should have been born with the caul.

In these early years, when I still assumed god placed us somewhere on his long agenda, I wondered if he had simply forgotten it when Simon was born, then sent it along with me as an after-thought, thinking it would at least arrive into the right family. Most say god never makes mistakes, but I was a reasonable child, able to accept that even as his powers outnumber ours, so must his list of responsibilities and details grow geometrically beyond our scope. I would cut him some slack.

But to assume the role of chosen one, in a family with my brother Simon—no, that I could never do.

Simon was the hero. Not just my hero. The hero, period. He couldn't have held his job any more decisively if he'd been born with the word tattooed on his forehead.

Now my sister DeeDee, she was the actress.

DeeDee's life fell apart the day Grandma Ginsberg called her a whore and a thief.

Mind you, this was nothing special.

Pushing into the depths of that back bedroom, you could be her loving grandchild, a wild Indian headhunter, or her whor-ing bastard ex-husband. Or perhaps the day would yield some new hallucination. Simon always smiled and took it philosophi-cally. I had long since stopped going in.

DeeDee stormed into the kitchen, where Simon and I sat at the table brushing sand paintings with salt we'd emptied from the shaker, her face red and hot with indignation, tears sliding through her toughest guard.

Simon grabbed her in a bear hug, and motioned me to come quickly, and we sandwiched her between us until the hitching of her sobs replaced trembling rage.

I felt the trembling, the hitch, and wondered why I couldn't feel pain and rage, as I appeared to be a sentient human, with nerve endings and everything.

"DeeDee," he said, "you know she always does this. Remem-ber when she called me *goyim* and slammed my hand in the door? That was way back when she was herself."

"I just can't stand it," DeeDee said, barely audible. "One grand-mother who hates me, fine—but not two for two."

He took her by the hand and we led her into my mother's room, where Mom lay half-sleeping, though it was after four. Simon ex-plained that Grandma Ginsberg had called DeeDee a whore and a thief. He knew and I knew that she did these things regularly, but for DeeDee's sake, I assumed, he filed an official report.

Our mother raised her head.

"Simon, did you get ground beef for dinner? Run to the store right now, dear."

"Mom," he repeated, "DeeDee is very upset."

"Make him grind it right in front of you. Don't get what's al-ready ground. God only knows what they put into that."

Blood rose into DeeDee's face again. "You don't listen, you crazy old lady," she screamed too close to my left eardrum.

"And hurry back from the store, dear—I'll get up and start dinner."

But she didn't move.

As Simon sprinted to the market clutching the dollar bill he had pulled from the grocery fund, DeeDee opened each of the kitchen cabinets, stood on a step stool, and hooked her arm be-hind every stack of dishes and glasses, pulling them out into gravity, and their appointment with the linoleum. When our mother ap-peared to start dinner, her slippered feet skidded around in the debris. I closed my eyes and pictured a beach scattered with a thou-sand clam shells, or a wind chime tinkling on the porch.

But a minute later, as she stood staring into the empty cabi-nets, the shards crunching under her weight, I imagined the sound my shattering teeth might make if I ever clenched them as hard as I really wanted.

After a few minutes' surveillance, and after Simon had re-turned, puffing from exertion, she turned back to him and asked if he'd remembered paper plates.

DeeDee would have screamed if in Simon's place. I would have groused that she'd requested no such thing. Simon simply pulled another dollar from the fund and took off running as my mother dropped the ground beef into an overheated pan with a startling sizzle.

No one thought about paper cups, and we had to take occasional trips from the table to the sink, to drink water from the faucet. We walked carefully to avoid slipping in the shifting sea of glass and china fragments.

Three days later I came home from school to find a box full of the stuff at the curb. I felt a great relief, knowing that my mother had noticed, even acknowledged, a situation requiring attention. The pleasure faded as my brother Simon pushed through the kitchen door with the second box. As I hung up my coat, he put the broom and dustpan away without comment.

"Simon, we don't have two grandmothers, do we?"

"Of course," he said. "Everybody has two grandmothers."

I knew there had been such a thing as a Grandma Sterling, but owing to the fact that I'd never seen her, I pictured her dead.

I asked why Grandma Sterling was never around, though it seemed like asking for trouble. If Grandma Ginsberg went away, I'd be smart enough not to inquire after her.

"Her choice," he said with a shrug, and then he whispered, "I don't think she likes us."

And what was my role in all of this? I had none. They'd all been taken. My job was not to exist at all. Though too much alive to play it to perfection, I feel I performed a fairly adept imitation.

EDGE OF THE EARTH

ON THE DRIVE to Sacramento, I question myself in an endless, hamster-wheel pattern as to whether Sarah thinks of herself as my brother's widow. Of course, I will not ask. Because if she does, I could no longer be kind to Sarah, and above all I need to be kind.

I arrive at the house late, too late, really. I can see I've awakened her. Her hair, fine and blond like his, flies in many directions, most leading across her face. Her fair skin seems lined and dough-like, the way his did upon waking. With my dark, Semitic looks, I'm sure an outsider would guess me as the wife, her as the sister. I suppose I'd switch with her if the world would allow.

She's glad to see me.

"Ella," she says. "Baby."

She's never called me baby before, but she's sleepy, a sort of inexpensive truth serum. And we are bound by a common love, a stronger bond now, as it extends to a common loss.

She throws her arms around me and I leech her warmth. It's not fair, really. It's a trick I learned from Grandma Ginsberg, to draw strength from an embrace without returning any. But I know Sarah will be warm in her house while I'm away, walking off the edge of a flat earth. I must assume she won't begrudge me.

She pulls me inside, where I tell her I want a complete lesson on where Simon's clothes were found.

Of course, I could have gotten that much by phone, but I need so much more. I need a piece of her to take along.

Then, I say, I will take a good night's sleep and proceed. But I do not take a good night's sleep.

I lie awake all night, on Simon's side of the bed, because there is only the one bedroom, thinking that I am no substitute for him, and have no right to be here.

The moon is nearly full, and a streak of it slides through his bedroom window, falling across the picture. Across Simon's soft, full cheeks, the fold of extra flesh under his chin, his sandy blond hair, which falls onto his forehead. He is a Tom Sawyer of a businessman. His mustache curls around at the corners of his smile. It is a twelve-year-old's smile. It always was. When he was seven, when he was forty.

The only thing my family ever did right was to breed that smile. The moon shows it all.

Thank god the moon is on my side. I'll need a piece of that, a piece of Sarah, all of myself and all of Simon. Even then, this may be the hardest thing I've ever done.

In the morning I am running on my generator.

Unlike some people, I function beautifully on no sleep, but a sort of auxiliary power kicks in, different from the natural one. It feels sharp-edged and cold. It tends to make people avoid me, even those who would be inclined to spend time around me to begin with.

Sarah does not avoid me.

She makes me a pot of coffee and a bacon omelet, and cries as she watches me eat.

She holds me at the door, as if she's on to me and knows what I need. She slips me more warm strength than I would think she could spare.

I walk across the street to my old pickup, like a hike across flat terrain to the edge of the earth.

THEN:

IF THE DRUMS had worked, I might still have a sister. The drums did not work.

It was a piece of clever thinking on DeeDee's part, though. I will grant her that.

By now, with Simon fifteen, DeeDee eleven, me nine, the age I accepted god's noninvolvement policy, my mother responded to almost nothing. Only one thing could rouse her out of bed: Grandma Ginsberg's heated complaints. Who would have thought such a thing could have a purpose?

DeeDee traded her bike for a set of drums, and, as a courtesy to the family, played them only in the garage. This broken-down structure, far too stacked and littered with yellowing sports sections to house the car, faced out onto the back yard, six feet from Grandma Ginsberg's window.

DeeDee never took lessons on the drums; she just pounded. Grandma Ginsberg screamed until her old throat faltered and her voice cracked into a hoarse whisper.

My mother did not get up.

Finally I asked Simon, who knew everything, why my mother would respond to nonsense from the old lady while ignoring a real problem.

"But that's just it," he said. "Don't you see?"

I wasn't sure I did, but I hated to appear ignorant in front of my brother.

In a few months the drums stood silent in the corner of the garage, near the spot where DeeDee took to setting fires. They were only little fires at first, but I sensed a personal game of chicken involved, as if she challenged herself to set a blaze which would tease the borderline of control.

When the big one came, Simon said it just got away from her by mistake. I'm sure he knew better, but he liked to think the best about people if they met him halfway.

The big one came at night, with DeeDee running through our room to Simon's room, yelling fire at the top of her lungs, as though this was news, her face blackened with smoke.

As my bare feet hit the cold boards of the bedroom floor, the room lit up like a night thunderstorm, only with lightning that stayed. I ran to the window to watch the flames engulf the garage roof. I heard Grandma Ginsberg come apart.

DeeDee climbed under my bed as Simon grabbed me by the shoulders.

"Call the fire department," he said.

I wished at that moment that I was Simon. Then I wouldn't have to ask a stupid question.

"Uh. What's their number again?"

"Just dial the operator. Tell her you need the fire department."

His blue eyes bored into me, full of fear, but a fear that wouldn't slow him down or trip him up.

As I told the fire department our address, I watched the trees rain, and the windows streak and flow with water. I ran outside to find Simon hosing down the roof.

Then it all happened at once, all the light, all the sound. The sirens blended with the popping wood, the cracking roof supports. The red flashing lights blended with the eerie flicker of the engulfed structure. Fire hoses overpowered Simon's little garden hose.

The neighborhood watched in robes and bare feet.

A fireman cornered my brother Simon. "Where are your parents, son?"

"My father's gone," I heard him say.

"Where's your mother?"

Simon only shrugged in that spooky glow. "I dunno. Sleeping, I guess." That's when it occurred to me that Grandma Ginsberg had fallen silent.

My mother was carried out of the house, against her will by the look of it. Simon informed the chief that DeeDee could be found under a bed.

The fire was quickly contained, though with no garage left to speak of; except for the scorched roof, the house sustained no real damage.

Grandma Ginsberg was carried out on a stretcher, her face covered with a sheet, already dead, I would learn later, of a heart attack.

I knew I would have my work cut out for me, wondering whether I needed to feel bad or not.

My mother stumbled back into the house on the all-clear signal, and fell asleep again, as Simon explained to the remaining firefighters that Grandma Ginsberg might have to be handled like a person with no relatives. Only Simon could explain a thing like that and cause grown men to nod their understanding.

Simon called Uncle Manny in the morning, and next thing we knew, our father was home, making all the arrangements.

Our mother did not attend the funeral. I felt sure her days were numbered now, or simply negated, so that even if they did drag on, they would go for nothing.

Our father asked Simon to say a few words to the bereaved.

"Just stand right up there, son, and say a few things you remember about your grandmother."

Simon did a lovely job, I thought.

He told the story of Grandma Ginsberg chasing DeeDee and him around the apartment, back in her mobile days, shaking her finger at them, saying "You dasn't do that" repeatedly over their laughter. He never explained their transgression, only the way they laughed at her later for her use of the word "dasn't," a word they could swear didn't exist in the English language.

Then he told the story of the slamming door. The day he saw baby DeeDee go into Grandma Ginsberg's bedroom and climb on the bed, and how he figured he could do it if she could. But then, when he tried, she called him *goyim* and held his hand in the bedroom door and slammed it on his hand to teach him better than to try such a thing again.

And then later he knew why, he explained, because he overheard her talking to our father, complaining that the Simon boy looked just like his *shiksa* wife.

As he explained this last little bit, Simon's voice faded as our father ushered him off the podium, away from the microphone.

Poor Simon. Poor brave, honest Simon. Everybody acted like he had a disease. He meant no harm, of course. Nobody had warned him that he was supposed to act.

DeeDee brought Andy, her stuffed horse, to the funeral, and to the *shiva*. She grabbed little handfuls of matzo strips or a piece of gefilte fish from the buffet, then hid under the coffee table, pretending to feed Andy.

If anyone had noticed, they might have found it odd behavior for a girl of eleven, but we were all three mercifully invisible, even our voices drowned in the moans and sobs.

I sat on the rug beside the coffee table, as though she'd let me be close to her. I reached out to pet Andy, but she slapped my hand away.

He was a small horse, six or seven inches long, stiff legs inside his blue and green cover to stand up by himself. Andy had a windup key in his belly, which my sister now cranked obsessively, causing him to roll his head around on a geared neck and play "Brahms' Lullaby."

Thinking I was being kind, I told DeeDee that when she grew up, she might be able to own a real horse.

She flew out from under the table at me, like ghosts from a Halloween house, threw me and pinned me and seized my throat in her adrenaline-powered grasp.

"Don't ever say Andy isn't a real horse. Ever. Promise."

I would have, if I could, if she had let go of my throat, or if Uncle Manny hadn't disrupted the moment by pulling her off to the other side of the room.

He sat with DeeDee on his lap, one huge arm around her waist, restraining her as she wailed and thrashed. He must have thought she was on her way back to attack me, but I knew better. I retrieved Andy from under the coffee table, and carried him, as reverently as I knew she would, back to his rightful owner. She sat still then.

It was the best apology I could make, because words would not have come close.

DeeDee didn't speak to me for a week. But she didn't speak to anyone else either, so I didn't take it too hard. Besides, she ended her silence in my presence, in our room just before sleep.

"If anything happens to me," she whispered, "I want you and Simon to give Andy a proper burial. With a funeral service and everything."

I wondered if we were to sit *shiva* for Andy, but I wasn't sure what I could say to her and what I couldn't.

"But Andy wouldn't be dead. Would he?"

"Of course he would. Without me? Absolutely he would. What would he be without me? No, without me, the only thing left for Andy is a decent burial."

I made my sister DeeDee a solemn promise.

When I woke the next day she was gone, to school I assumed, and Andy was a lump under the edge of my pillow.

Mom didn't notice when DeeDee forgot to come home. Simon said she ran away, but he knew better, I think. He liked to think the best.

I told him about Andy, about the promise, and we found a flashlight and set out around bedtime, sorting a careful grid on the three-acre woodlot behind our house until we found her.

I was glad I couldn't see Simon's face as we stood beneath that tree, flashlight drooped in his hand, listening to the sickening creak of rope on tree limb as the breeze blew through.

I asked my brother Simon if we call the fire department for something like this.

DO NOT CROSS

I LOCATE MY approximate goal by landmark. The sun glares into my unblinking eyes, and I pull my hat brim down to shield them. I probably should think I'm standing someplace beautiful.

The hill slopes away beneath my feet, the grass winter green, the sky a perfect cloudless blue contrast. Everywhere I look I see trees. I have never been fond of trees. Well, not never, but not for a long time.

Now I see a small brown rabbit. He stares at me. I stare back. I take a step toward him, thinking he will run. He holds his ground, staring. He turns, lopes a few rabbit steps away, and looks over his shoulder at me.

I walk the other way.

It's the hawk that turns me back again, away from the direction I think I should travel.

He spreads his great patterned wings and glides from tree to tree, and I trot along, afraid, as always, that life will happen too fast and I will be left behind.

I catch my foot and go sprawling.

I scrape my chin on a rock, and as it bleeds onto my shirt, I notice it's a strip of wood that snagged me. Not a natural strip, as one might expect out here, but a carefully cut and milled piece of narrow lumber, sticking straight up out of the ground.

I stand, wipe my chin on my shoulder and stamp the grass down all around my find.

I walk a pattern, rolling out in ever-widening circles until I find another. I clear the grass aside to discover a knot of plastic tape still attached, as if the remainder had been carelessly torn away, with a little tail flapping in the breeze.

The tail contains bits of faded words: DO NOT CR

Within minutes I've paced off the four corners of the site. The fourth stick also contains a strip of police tape. It says: LINE DO N

I remember the first time I ever saw my brother Simon cry. We stood under a scrub oak, something like the one above me now, holding the little board box Simon had made for Andy. We were affording Andy his promised proper burial, the day after the police tape disappeared from around that tree.

"How do you cry, Simon?"

I was so in awe of him, the things he could do that seemed like foreign currency to me. Shoot baskets. Bench press seventy pounds. Cry.

"I don't know," he said, wiping his eyes and nose on his sleeve. "You just do."

I bend now to touch the sun-bleached scrap of tape, afraid to walk into the rectangle of my brother's misfortune.

How do you cry, Ella? You just do. But my stomach is tight, my head tingly, my eyes dry, and I just don't.

I step inside, to the center of the area, now clean of my brother's clothes, long since entered into evidence when a scruffy rider of the rails found himself in custody for attempting to pass Simon's checks.

I sit down hard to ease my dizziness. The hawk screams at me.

I feel a sense of lightness, which is very much what I feared. I feel a release, an end to worldly tension, to remorse. I feel a letting go. I suppose this could mean two things. Simon has left this world. Or, wherever he is, Simon is happy.

If Simon has left this world, I will walk off the edge soon enough myself.

I hear DeeDee's voice in my head, as I have often since Simon's disappearance, as if she must speak louder with only one sibling to listen.

She says, *but you wouldn't be dead. Would you?* Of course I would. Without Simon? Absolutely I would. What would I be without Simon?

I decide that, wherever Simon is now, he is happy.

THEN:

OUR MOTHER ATTENDED the funeral only because our father dressed and dragged her. He stood in the middle of her bedroom, supported her around the waist with one arm and slipped a black dress over her head with his free hand.

We only peeked in for brief moments at a time, skittering back and forth from living room to bedroom, wondering which was the worse spot to light.

In the living room was our father's lady friend, and both halves of that term only loosely applied to Sheila, transfixed by the task of polishing her nails. She wore her hair piled on her head like an exotic dancer or a waitress, her skirt too short. Long after our father had loaded Mom into the passenger seat of his new car, Simon and I respectfully silent in the back seat, I pictured Sheila, long legs crossed, extending one hand with spread fingers, blowing on the wet polish.

"Isn't this a lovely day for a wedding, Gabe?" our mother chirped as he pulled away from the curb.

"We're not going to a wedding, Betty, we're going to our daughter's funeral."

She turned her face to him, showing us her warm smile in profile. "This will be just like old times for us, won't it, Gabe?"

She patted his cheek.

Our father said nothing, just shot Simon a sidewise glance, as if my brother had intentionally withheld details of our mother's decline, as if it had always been Simon's job to keep the measurements and tell the tales.

I retained only one detail of DeeDee's memorial service. I felt I should remember every nuance as a way of proving I would never become my mother.

But only this one moment remained.

The rabbi, standing before the bereaved, announced that we gathered to mourn the tragic loss of Deborah Naomi Ginsberg.

Simon and I exchanged a glance.

Nobody, but nobody, called DeeDee "Deborah," despite the fact that it was her given name. In DeeDee's world, people could be maimed for lesser transgressions.

There was a time when I truly believed that I stood and offered the proper correction aloud, with such firm authority that the rabbi could hardly do other than to apologize to our sister's lost soul. I ran it by Simon years later, who informed me, with tenderness, that we both sat frozen and lifeless, and uttered not so much as a peep.

I felt engulfed in hopelessness at that moment on my sister DeeDee's behalf. Imagine DeeDee, of all people, forced to lie in a box and endure such insult without recourse. Surely death is the most helpless and irrevocable of states.

Simon cried. My father wiped his own eyes in nervous, twitchy little motions, as if he might dissociate from the action. My mother clutched his arm, or knee, or both, gazing at him lovingly.

Beyond that, I remember only a mental veil, a kind of blankness, like the white noise of after-hours television before the test pattern arrives.

Later that night, long after ten, Simon and I crawled out onto the roof of our house, through the attic window and on into the night, and stared across the wreckage.

We perched at the apex, carefully straddling the shingled slopes for balance, and the moon sat in its own yellowish glow on the horizon.

Our mother's ancient Studebaker stood where it always stood, parked at the curb, collecting pine needles, waiting for nothing. The cracked, charcoaled support beams that had once been our garage lay at crazy angles, shiny in their blackness.

Beyond this stretched the three-acre woodlot, its trees appearing more twisted, more darkly gnarled than before, like the netherworlds and dark forests of fantasy tales I wouldn't read for years to come.

"Nothing seems very different, Simon, does it?"

He didn't answer, and I heard the question ring back through my ears and wondered if I understood it myself. Everything was different. Yet somehow, in a way I couldn't explain, I wanted the loss of DeeDee to change something that appeared unchanged. Maybe I wanted the moon to stop in its orbit, or the day never to arrive. Maybe I wanted to be a different person without her, instead of what I was, myself, only more beaten, less direct.

Just for a moment I wanted Andy back. Though I knew I'd never defile his grave, I felt pinched between her wishes and my own desire to hold on.

"Nothing will ever be the same," he said at last.

"But if we just go on, like we're doing," I said, "then why was she even here? If she can just be subtracted, what was she? Why did she even go to all the trouble?"

Simon turned half around and slid down the roof a ways to rest his back at an angle against the slope, his knees bent, feet braced for stability, his head dropped back to face the stars.

I did the same.

"We'll keep her with us," he said.

An outsider, overhearing this remark, might have taken it as a bland, sappy comment about the dead living on in the hearts of those who loved them. That wasn't what he meant. Simon and I spoke in a kind of shorthand.

From that moment, DeeDee would exist between us in a freak-ishly tangible way. We would consult her before making decisions, talk and listen to her with respect, leave room for her in all physical spaces and in every personal exchange.

I comforted myself by thinking that this did not make us at all like our mother, because, unlike her, we recognized the arrangement as a poor second. We admitted it to be a fractional salvage of loss.

Our father stayed the night, packed Sheila into a cab the following morning and sent her away alone.

He picked up the telephone receiver and left it glued to his ear, only pressing the button to hang up between calls.

I sat on the landing of the stairs with my brother Simon, magically relieved of our responsibility to school, which I suppose was something of what I wanted in suggesting that morning had no right to come. We listened to every conversation, and although cryptic, heard only from his end, a pattern emerged.

"Yes, Manny," our father would say, "it's worse than I thought. No, worse than that. No, nobody said a word to me—the kids never said a thing. No wonder it was such a strain on the girl, god keep her. . . . Well, I know, Manny, but I'm her ex-husband. I know that, but I'm the children's father. Well, somebody has to— that's my point, that's all I'm really trying to say. . . . No, I called her long distance. She hung up on me, that's what. Like this is a big surprise. Then I called back but she wouldn't answer. You know how much she hates me. You know what she said to me, Manny? Before she hung up? Before I could even tell her what I'd called to say, Manny? She said, 'What daughter? I have no daughter'. . . . I know—that's exactly what I said. But you know what she's like. . . . Not living, no. . . . Well, somebody has to, that's my point. That's all I'm trying to say. . . . Well, me, of course. I mean, somebody has to take care of them. They're kids. They can't raise themselves."

My brother Simon and I stared into each other's eyes, and at the walls, alternately, feeling a sense of the unspoken factor, searching for some clarification of it in our mutual understanding.

Then a number of additional calls, in a tone more formal.

"I'm calling to inquire about your facility. . . . Well, how much of that would the state pay. . . ? I see."

In the morning he sat us down, said our mother had a sickness that didn't show. Didn't show, I thought. You don't spend much time around here. But I maintained a measured silence.

We were not invited to come along for the ride.

Uncle Manny—big, hearty, unflappable Uncle Manny—came to stay with us while our father flew home to pack and ship his belongings.

While we waited, we bundled and hauled stacks of sports sections to the front yard. If we had cared to, we could have stacked them high enough to obscure the house from the street, but we only made a series of loose mounds, which happy Boy Scouts dragged away.

Simon and I moved into a common room in the attic, because my father felt comfortable in the privacy afforded by owning the entire second floor.

We'd lie in bed at night and wonder aloud about the safety, indeed the purpose, of asking where our mother had been taken, and whether or not visits could be arranged.

DeeDee said we should be smart for a change, and ask no questions at all.

In just a matter of weeks, our new way of life sketched itself out in painful detail, leaving no room for confusion. We decided without prearrangement that DeeDee's opinions were the most solid of the three, and should be accepted as a tiebreaker, or in any situation in which stress or doubt might cloud our limited, living vision.

Our father installed a lock on the outside of the attic door to assure we would not stumble downstairs after lights out.

Night after night we collected auditory data.

The front door opening and closing long after midnight, too many times a night. Voices, always strange, never overlapping. Three, four, five new voices all at once. Sounds—human, we assumed, though some frighteningly close to the border between human and animal, between pleasure and pain. Laughter. Bed springs. Or couch springs. A gentle trying of our door. Because, you see, our father had installed a real deadbolt, not just a hook on the outside of the door, but a lock that we could not open from the inside, and that no one on the outside could open, except our father with his key.

"Well, Ella," Simon said one night, "you said you wanted everything to change."

As is so often the case, by the time I realized that my wish had been answered, it was far too late for retraction.

THE EVE OF SETTING OFF

IN A DUSTY corner of a defunct service station, near a wall of treadless tires, I phone Raphael from a phone booth out of sight and earshot of every living thing except me—and the pieces of people I've carried along.

"Ella." His voice clarifies my reasons for calling. "I didn't think I'd hear from you again."

"Well, you might not," I say. "After this."

I want to tell him that my new earth is dry, the sky too wide. I want to tell him I know what I have to do now, but it's hard. Because I can't take any comfort with me, not even my friendly old truck, which is why I need the comfort of his voice on the eve of setting off.

Instead I say, "I've decided Simon's alive." I don't know that he is, I've simply decided it, and I'm sure Raphael hears that in my voice, although he knows me well enough to guess it. "I've decided he walked out of this place on his own feet."

"Naked?"

"Naked? I don't know. Maybe. Or in a change of clothes."

Raphael doesn't ask why my brother would do that, which is a blessing, because there's no reason I can offer. Still, I've decided. For a moment Raphael asks nothing at all, and I watch the hot wind swirl a weak dust devil in the brown, empty soil of nowhere.

Then he says, "So what will you do?"

"I'll start walking," I say, as if it's so simple I can't imagine the need to spell it out.

"Good luck," he says, but I hear what he doesn't say, too. Still, you can't judge a man by what he doesn't say, even if you can hear it.

"I love you, Raphael."

"I know that. I never doubted that, Ella."

I touch the phone lightly back to its receiver, as if afraid of a spark at contact.

I climb into the old truck for the last time and head into the dusk. Before I park it one final time, I wish it a good life. I wish for it to be stolen by someone who needs it, and I leave the keys.

I take only the pocketknife that Simon gave me when I was eleven, a sleeping bag with one change of clothes rolled inside, toothbrush, comb, a small picture of Simon, and all the money I own. I also bring Simon, a piece of Sarah, DeeDee, and what's left of myself, but these things don't weigh me down.

I camp the night within the rectangle of stakes and ask my dreams to point me.

I have no dreams.

I clutch the sleeping bag around my neck in the night, awakened from time to time by a sharp, chill wind across my cheek. The ground pinches my hip and I toss around.

In the morning I am hungry and thirsty, and I have no plans for these needs. In fact, I have no plans.

I lie still as long as I can, and I notice a brown rabbit watching me from under a bush. The same rabbit, or another one, I don't know. This land must contain a million rabbit lookalikes.

When the hawk screams I sit up.

I watch him perch in the tree above me and crook his neck to stare, watch his round black eye contain me doubtfully. Still, I think he doubts me less than I doubt myself.

He glides away on a cushion of air, and I stand and take a few steps after him, and as I do, I am surer than ever that my brother Simon continued from this place.

My challenge is to continue in the same direction.

The hawk lights in a tree and waits while I pack my only remaining physical symptoms of life.

THEN:

ONE ADVANTAGE TO living with our father was a freedom to stay home from school unnoticed. We'd trudge out of the house at the regular hour and head anywhere else. He'd set off for work a minute later, leaving us free to come home, usually to take the sleep we missed at night. Simon forged beautiful notes.

On Jewish holidays we simply slept in.

"Why aren't you in school?" he'd say when we came down to breakfast.

"It's Yom Kippur."

"You don't go to temple, you should go to school."

Here, oddly, I played spokesperson.

"Wouldn't make a difference. They mark us absent all the same."

"Why would they do that?"

"They just go down the list and mark us all off. Feinberg, Greenberg, Goldman, Ginsberg. You have to jump around like crazy to make them see you're there."

Unfortunately, I was not making this up.

"Well, think reverent thoughts," he would say, seeming not to notice that we stuffed ourselves with pancakes on the holy fast day of the Jewish religion.

If the days were good, the nights brought the bill.

I tried to avoid liquids after six, I tried to cross my legs and will it away, but the only solution was to cut me loose to sprint to the bathroom one floor down.

Simon found the answer to this most immediately distressing problem, and it came in the form of a well-devised rope ladder hooked to two heavy eye bolts in the floor of our attic bedroom, under the window.

If we remembered to unlock the window underneath us before bed, the ladder released me off the side of the roof into the dangerous second-floor night.

I had to remember not to flush.

The first few times Simon came along as a sort of bodyguard, assuming the jungle of the hall would be thick with danger, but it invariably proved empty. The sounds came from the living room. The activity, so real beneath us, had actually been two floors down all the time, disguising its voice to imitate a dark creature breathing a heartbeat away.

In time I was allowed to go alone, and I must say I felt nothing shameful at first in the fact that I was drawn to look. The second-floor landing loomed and invited. It served as a duck blind, its thick, close-set railing posts obscuring my presence, its darkness a contrast to the harsh lights on the downstairs stage.

The first time, I stared so long that Simon launched a search party. He found me crouched, remorseless, full of words and questions, but afraid to break the sheltering silence.

Then Simon had to stare awhile, too.

My father sat sprawled on the couch, naked, a huge, unfathomable appendage leaning tautly against his belly.

This is not to say that I had no understanding of the concept of a penis, but this one surely pushed the concept to remarkable dimensions.

Two other strange naked figures knelt on the floor beneath him, faced away from us, their mouths wetly attached to separate portions of this gigantic member.

When tired of marveling at the amazing thing itself, I watched my father's eyes, rolled back in his head, showing the whites of surrender, and listened to the unearthly rumble of his wordless commentary.

I drew from him the sense of a power he held at no other time, a mastery of moments that would cause grown people to follow him home, this stranger, this normally bland and ineffectual everyman.

Simon took a proprietary hold on my arm and ushered me up the side of the house for the night.

He couldn't usher away my questions.

"Have you ever seen one that big, Simon? I mean, is that normal?"

Simon offered no opinions, careful to stress no real basis for comparison, other than himself, or other boys his age he might be forced to shower beside.

"Do you think that's why he wants everyone to see it, Simon?"

Simon couldn't imagine why he'd want that. Simon had reached the modest phase, closing himself into the closet to change into his pajamas in our room at night. He could find no explanation for a grown man, for any man, to intentionally bare himself to a stranger.

"Were those both girls down there, Simon? One of them was awfully hairy."

"I don't know," he said, folding his pillow around his head. "I don't want to know. I wish you would go to sleep."

I stopped asking questions, but I did not go to sleep.

In fact, I tossed out Simon's carefully knotted skeleton key and released myself back into the jungle, where I crouched, wide-eyed, long into the night.

I watched my father lie across the prone back of one figure, the one I became increasingly convinced was no woman, and saw, as if by cheap sleight of hand, my father's great appendage disappear, though I could not imagine where it might have gone. Well, no, I could imagine, but that was all I could do. I could not confirm my own unlikely conjectures.

Meanwhile the female body coiled behind them, her head pressed into that confusing juncture, finding some contact, some purpose, I assumed, that I was simply too naïve or too far away to understand.

I knelt before the show again the following night, and the night after that, feeling a mental and physical tingle which I liked and hated, sensing a lesson in progress that I must study, that I would later need. Just as I forced a first-grader to teach me the alphabet before my promotion from kindergarten, I assumed that the information would prove requisite without notice, that the test might precede the lesson.

By the second time Simon came down to catch me, I felt ready to practice on my own.

"Look, Simon," I said, the faintest of whispers into his soft, pale ear, "look what she's doing." I referred to a woman, so far as I could tell, one of four in attendance, who forced a meager portion of my father's penis into her mouth in strange, heated rhythms. "You want to try that?"

My eagerness sounded childish, beneath even my ten years of experience, unguarded.

I leaned into him so hard that I toppled him, and myself across him, onto the worn carpet of the landing.

Simon sat up, pushed me off him, wrestled me around to the banister again, clutching me so tight around the waist that I could hardly pull a full breath.

"Is that what you want to be, Ella?" he hissed in my ear, venomous as I never thought Simon would or could be. "You want to grow up to be one of those? An animal?" On the word *animal*, his angry tone rang out sharp and strong, our father's eyes shot up to the landing, and he flew to his feet, pulling Grandma Ginsberg's hand-crocheted afghan off the back of the sofa to cover himself. Loosely woven and full of round, patterned openings, it proved a singularly unfortunate choice.

By the time he got upstairs, we'd climbed back to the attic. I don't believe he ever witnessed our means of escape. He did not come in after us, though we could hear him usher all guests out the door.

We spent days, weeks, waiting for the long talk from our father, which never came. He simply learned to father us loosely, distantly, without benefit of eye contact.

The house fell quiet, the nights uneventful. If visitors came by night, they came too quietly to wake us.

Sleep became an easy and natural way to spend the dark hours.

A near year passed in this no man's land of trouble, not joyous by any means, but lacking immediate, pressing pain.

Then some evidence of activity recurred, though it recurred quietly. If not for the click of the front door latch, we might have suspected nothing at all. Simon found a big kitchen pot to keep under my bed, and commandeered a roll of toilet paper, to help me through the long nights.

I would not have gone downstairs even if I had dared, owing to my decision, with the youthful finality of a floodgate snapping shut against pressure, that I would not grow up to be an animal.

This was Simon's doing, and none of my own.

About this time DeeDee began to give advice.

Just go, she would say. *Just get out.*

But Simon, now seventeen, and I, just eleven, could not imagine it. We would never question DeeDee's wisdom, but, go where? Eat what? Stay safe how?

No, surely that was easy for DeeDee to say.

And it was funny, about the things DeeDee would say. I never heard them, at least, not in these early years. No voices talked in my ears. Simon and I never compared notes as to what thoughts we would credit to her presence.

We simply talked out our reactions to her suggestions, never worrying that our perceptions might differ, never questioning their source.

I started to talk about going to see Grandma Sterling, maybe living with her. Simon would shake his head with sad resignation.

"You heard what Dad said. She says she doesn't even have a daughter. So how could she have grandchildren?"

"But, with us right on her doorstep and all. How could she not have grandchildren?"

I thought she'd be forced to admit our existence almost by default, but DeeDee said *fat chance*.

For over a year we talked, planned, just the three of us, arrived at no conclusions, took no steps toward leaving.

Then one night our father failed to come home and lock us in at all.

Simon and I sat on the roof most of the night, thinking it a safe vantage point from which to watch him arrive, which he did not. When I got so sleepy that Simon worried I'd tumble off, we climbed back inside to sleep.

Our father phoned the following morning, a little before six. He'd been arrested, he said, and since he had only this one phone call, it was important that Simon contact Sol, our father's lawyer, as soon as he hung up the phone.

This part Simon told me later.

At the time I heard only Simon's end of the exchange.

"Well, when are you coming home, then...? You have to come home sometime.... But you never go to jail.... Oh. Well, how long could they keep you...? Oh. Can we come visit you...? With strangers, though? Will they let us stay together?"

My stomach clenched in acidic knots and DeeDee reminded me that I couldn't say she hadn't warned us. We should have just gotten out, worried later about the where and how.

Simon hung up the phone, his face slack and bloodless.

"He's going to have the prison people call the child welfare department. We'll have to go live somewhere else."

"Together?"

"If they can. If somebody'll take us both."

Simon looked at me, I looked at Simon, and nothing more was said, or needed to be.

We began our packing, knowing without discussion the importance of traveling light.

WALKING THROUGH WALLS

THE FIRST FIFTEEN miles are the hardest, because I think I can't walk this far. My feet blister, but I keep walking. The blisters break and drain into my socks, but I walk.

Every step brings pain, so I force myself to remember the time when I loved pain, followed it, thought it would cleanse me, right my wrongs. Only half sure that my brother Simon is still with us, it isn't hard to project back to that time.

At about fifteen miles, and of course I am guessing, I hit a wall. I can't go another step. I walk through it, and the fact that I can go no further becomes irrelevant.

I welcome the pain like my own flesh and blood. Brain disengaged, legs working like pistons, I walk at least another five.

Then I notice it's getting dark, which seems unreasonable. Looking up across the sky, I think I hear the hawk scream, but I can't see him. I see the sun, high overhead, and then I know. This darkness doesn't belong to the night. It belongs to me.

DeeDee says she doesn't know why I should be surprised. Without Simon I never would have pulled out of the tunnel to begin with.

However, I am not surprised, nor can I push myself to feel great concern. If Simon were here, right here, I'd mind the tunnel a lot more, because Simon wants me to be sane, and he worked so hard for it. If he's gone forever it hardly matters. If he's gone for now I have time to work it out.

I stop and look around. Everywhere I look I see only what's in front of me. I'm losing my periphery. I see no town, no signs of life. Just a mountain, then another. I wonder how much longer

I'll walk before finding a town. Fifty miles? A hundred? I drop into a sit.

I pull off my shoes and socks, my first amateur's mistake, and the breeze stings my hot, open blisters. I prop my feet up on my rolled sleeping bag and lie on my back staring at the sky, which is moving away from me, fading to a dullness like the world through night vision glasses.

I could die out here, and worse yet, it doesn't matter.

I realize I am nowhere, near nothing, in touch with nothing. I don't even know which part of nowhere I've located. I think of my days on the road with Simon, and I know I should have felt the same thing. Both then and now I've succeeded in placing my body where my head is, performing a literal version of my own emotional state. Except then I had Simon, and it was fine.

Simon! I shout in the enforced quiet of my brain. I want him to see me, so I can see. Only Simon really sees me when I'm invisible. Simon and maybe for a minute Mrs. Hurley, but she's long gone.

Then again, I think, so is DeeDee.

On that note DeeDee sticks in her two cents' worth. *You haven't asked me my opinion about all this.*

"No, that's right," I say out loud. "I haven't. What do you think I should do, DeeDee?"

Keep walking.

"Do you think Simon's alive?"

I figure she of all people should know. But suddenly she has nothing to say, which is unlike DeeDee.

I try to put my shoes back on, but my feet have swelled to new limits in their sudden freedom, and the shoes no longer fit.

Simon didn't have shoes, DeeDee says. *He walked in his bare feet.*

So I do that, leaving shoes and socks behind to mark the spot where I gave up the game again.

I am filled with a new sense of hope, the thought that I will find my way now, because the soles of my feet will know things about where I must go. I decide that walking in shoes was like walking blindfolded, and if there's one thing I don't need, it's additional limits on my vision. The sky is out of range, but I don't mind.

THEN:

THREE WEEKS BEFORE Simon's seventeenth birthday our mother's old brown Studebaker had disappeared from its new resting place in front of the square of black concrete, where, by our father's arrangement, the garage rubble had been suitably razed and cleared.

On Simon's birthday the car had reappeared, its engine freshly overhauled, its sun-bleached surface waxed to a questionable sheen, its registration redone in Simon's name, all part of a long campaign to ace fatherhood, to repurchase our approval. Simon said Dad was a model of patience during the driving lessons. If so, he must have pasted it on.

On the day my father was arrested, we packed the trunk full of carefully weeded necessities, eyeing its leftover space on every load, to judge what percentage of two lives it might accommodate. As if by prearrangement, we packed nothing into the back seat other than pillows and blankets. We would need that space. Because without hitchhikers, our gasoline fund would die young.

Simon rummaged through the house, through drawers, through my father's pockets, the various petty cash funds in crocks on the kitchen counter, gathering forty-two dollars and twenty cents.

He made sure I brought towels, soap and toothpaste, none of which had crossed my mind at any time. He brought Grandma Sterling's address.

"Just in case," he said. "Who knows? We might just drop in and say hello."

As he pulled the car smoothly onto the highway I asked when he'd last seen Grandma Sterling.

"I never saw her."

"Ever?"

"DeeDee and I wrote her a letter one time, but it came back unopened."

"Didn't that make you feel terrible, Simon?"

"Well, not too bad. Mom wrote her, back when Mom had that cancer surgery. You probably don't remember that. You were just a baby. And Grandma Sterling never wrote back. To her own daughter. When she was afraid she might die. So I figure, I'm a stranger, why should I feel bad?"

I nursed a little pocket of queasiness thinking we might actually go there and see her face to face. But then I looked down the endless stretch of highway and decided not to borrow trouble from too far down the road. Just getting from California to Pennsylvania presented problems to keep us busy for now.

The first hitchhiker we picked up was Earl. We stopped for him at night, on a stretch of California desert. Earl wore pants a few inches too short, and a three- or four-day growth of beard. The whole car smelled like him immediately. He said he was going as close to Las Vegas as we cared to take him.

He asked if we had any money, in a way that made Simon uncomfortable. I could tell.

"We know as much about bad luck as you do, Earl. With what we just spent on gas, our life savings amounts to a little over thirty-six dollars."

"Hand it over then," Earl said.

Simon handed a five dollar bill over the seat. "Here's five to ease your situation, Earl. But if I give you all of it, we're as good as dead out here. Try to understand. We'll drive you all the way to Las Vegas, because we may as well go that way as any other, but we need gas money to do that, Earl."

"Look, I've got a knife." He pulled it from his pocket as he said this, but Simon, with his eyes on the road, didn't see. Earl never opened out the blade.

DeeDee cut in right about then.

Tell him he won't hurt us. That's what I heard DeeDee say. So I said, "I know you're not going to hurt us, Earl." Because just hearing it from DeeDee would not likely be good enough for Earl.

"Oh yeah? Why the hell shouldn't I? What are you to me?"

"Why?" I heard Simon ask. I wondered if he was thinking out loud or questioning DeeDee.

Because he's too decent a man, DeeDee said.

"Because you're a decent man, Earl," I said, in case Simon hadn't heard. "Just down on your luck is all. And because you know we'd never hurt you."

Simon waved the five dollar bill to call attention to his offering.

I watched Earl's eyes, illuminated in the lights of westbound traffic, thinking of the spark wheels we used to play with in our genuine youth. I'd like to say I was afraid, but I wasn't, not really, because Earl was obviously just a scared child, like any other desperate man.

Earl cried. He took the five dollars out of my brother's hand and threw the knife onto the front seat.

"Here, this is worth five dollars."

Simon thanked him and gave the knife to me as a gift. "That's good," Earl said. "She should have that. Not safe to be a young girl anymore. Not like it used to be. You can just pull over anywhere and drop me."

"Don't you want to ride on to Las Vegas?"

The sparks had gone from Earl's eyes, and he averted them as if we'd somehow become his superiors, as if he felt unworthy.

"You ain't gonna take me to Vegas after I tried to stick you up."

But of course we did, dropping him on the main drag just before sunrise, wishing him the best of luck turning five into a million. The neon of the hotels and casinos flooded the night like a diamond bracelet in the sun, at this of all hours.

I asked Simon if he'd been scared.

"Of course. Weren't you?"

I told him I was, because I didn't want him to know I'd forgotten how to feel. If I was becoming more like our mother, I didn't want to burden him with it now, when he had so much else on his mind.

On the way out of town we picked up Mrs. Hurley, a thin, frail old black woman with a thick braid of gray hair and a mouth full of jumbled teeth.

"Why, thank you, children," she said in a sweet accent as she settled her lean old bones onto the back seat. "Poor old woman like to freeze out there in this desert. Can't believe that bus driver begrudge an old lady some medicine for her arth-er-itis."

She pulled a flask from inside her cloth coat and pulled a short swallow.

"He made you get off the bus?"

"Well, not the first time. First time he just took it away. But I got two, see, 'cause you never know. Second time he says, lady, I just cut you all the slack I can cut by law. And he set me by the side of the road. Can you imagine? I says to him, I says, somebody ought to be nicer to your grammy, and I hope they do. But he just drove on. You shoulda heard the names I called his momma after that."

I squirmed all the way around in my seat to watch Mrs. Hurley's face. When she saw me watching, she smiled at me. It was a kind of smile I'd never seen before. Easy and real, as though it required no planning. Every one of her teeth seemed to point in a different direction, but no matter how hard they tried, they couldn't make that smile any less beautiful.

It made my stomach tingle. I worked on smiling at her, so she'd smile back. But it was an effort for me, a trip into the unfamiliar. It made me think of the tin man in *The Wizard of Oz*, getting his mouth oiled because he'd been left out in the field too long, to rust.

Mrs. Hurley asked our names, and why we were out in this cold, difficult world alone.

I watched Simon's face change, watched the thoughts at work behind his eyes, deciding. Then he told her the whole truth about our parents.

"Sometimes it makes you wonder," she said, "why the Lord would choose to balance so much on young shoulders. Must be because the young are so strong. Not rigid strong, but strong like a green stick."

DeeDee said, *good theory, lady.* But of course Mrs. Hurley couldn't hear.

Then Simon told her we were going to see our grandmother, who we'd never met, and who might or might not want to see us. Mrs. Hurley said she couldn't imagine a woman on god's green earth who wouldn't be pleased to meet her own grandchildren.

Simon drove silent for a mile or more. Then he said, "She doesn't like us because we're half Jewish."

"Ah," Mrs. Hurley said, "there's something I know and can understand. You wanta know something about me? I'm only three-quarters Negro. My father's father was a white man. You think anybody cares? You think anybody gives me a quarter the respect they pay a white woman? No, sir."

At a rest stop somewhere in northeast Arizona I woke in the morning to find Simon sitting on the hood of the Studebaker, and Mrs. Hurley snoring in the back seat, her cheek flattened against the glass.

I stepped out into the chilly desert morning to sit with Simon. I stared where he stared, at a red-brown mesa, stretching on forever, whittled and designed by eons of wind. I watched my brother's eyes, knowing he saw something I didn't.

"What does it look like to you, Simon?"

"Almost like god."

I figured that Simon, damn near eighteen, must be close enough to god to see him in the distance like light at the end of a tunnel.

"Go in the ladies' room and wash up," he said. "And put on clean clothes and comb your hair. That's important. If we don't, we'll look like hoboes, and that's like sending a signal to everybody that we don't respect ourselves. So then, why should they?"

I cleaned and groomed myself carefully, and when I came out, I found Simon still staring at the godlike mesa.

Mrs. Hurley bought us breakfast and a tank of gas, and we offered to drive her right to her doorstep in Columbus.

Halfway across the Texas panhandle, we had to stop over a whole night for Simon to catch up on his sleep.

Mrs. Hurley and I, who slept whenever we wanted, sat out on a bench in the starry night. I made a game of seeing how many times I could get her to smile.

"Isn't Texas just the flattest place on earth," she said, wrapping me against her in her huge coat.

I looked around, saw nothing to break the landscape but the rest station bathrooms, a building in the midst of nothing like the manger in the nativity. The stars seemed to surround us in wide-angle, as if we lived inside the dome of a snow globe.

"I've heard it said there's more stars in Texas than anywhere else in the world," she said. "You know, he's a fine young man, your Simon."

I smiled without trying. "You know what my sister DeeDee says? She says insanity runs in our family, but it jumps over Simon."

Mrs. Hurley laughed, a light, ringing sound, like something that would come naturally with the spring.

"I think it mighta given you a clean miss too, little Ella."

"Oh, no. Not me. Only Simon." Then: "Mrs. Hurley? Do you think maybe our grandmother really doesn't want to know us at all?"

Mrs. Hurley hugged me tighter to her bony side. "Well, now, honey, maybe she just thinks she doesn't. Because maybe she just doesn't know yet what fine young people you grew up to be."

"That's a good answer, Mrs. Hurley."

We sat alone under the great dome of lights, allowing ourselves to be ever so much smaller than the world until Simon woke up.

THE NAKED MAN

THE HAWK SCREAMS, and light spills into my tunnel, dispersing it. I squint, then press my eyes shut for relief. When I open them I see a town.

More significantly, I am standing barefoot on a spot my brother Simon has crossed. For the first time since the start of my wanderings, I have chanced across a piece of my target.

I am pleased with myself for knowing this.

The town spreads out a mile or so below me, but the back door of the nearest house is practically in my lap. I stand facing a board fence where, just the other side, a fiftyish woman in a denim shirt and sun hat and heavy work gloves prunes roses.

The hawk screams again. I look up to see him above her yard in a tree, watching me with agitation. I wonder why the woman does not look up. Maybe the hawk is not really there. Or maybe I'm not. I could be invisible. It's happened before.

I take two steps toward her fence. My movement catches her eye; she looks at my face, questioning at first, then she smiles.

"Good morning," she says. "You took a nasty scrape there."

My hand flies to my chin, a band of cracked scab. I'd forgotten, although it hurts. I pull the photo from my bedroll.

"I'm looking for my brother Simon," I say, and show it to her. "I thought you might have seen him."

She studies the picture longer than necessary. She likes him, I can tell. Everybody likes Simon. She's thinking that if she had lost someone like that, she'd want him back, too. I can see that in her face.

I want to tell her that my brother Simon used to be a gardener, years ago, but I am just lucid enough to know she doesn't care about that.

"I can't say that I have."

"His clothes were found twenty or twenty-five miles west of here. I thought he might have come by this way."

"Clothes?" she asks. "You think he might have come by here without them?"

"Well, it's unlike him. But it's hard to know what to think."

"Unless he was the naked man. But that was over two months ago."

"The naked man?"

"Well, he wasn't naked, really. He had on jockey shorts. Walked down off the hill, just like you did now, then on toward town."

"Was he a blond man, like my brother?"

She shakes her head. "Too far away to tell. Didn't care to get too close to him, you know. We all thought . . . well, we weren't sure what to think."

"Who else saw him?"

"Seems like nobody except my neighbor. We think he's the one stole that pair of overalls down off Mr. Mobley's clothesline. Because a naked man in town—now that would've turned a few heads."

I want to know which neighbor. She says the one who's in Chicago just now. No, no emergency number. "She didn't say if he was blond, only that his forehead and arms were all blistered from sunburn and he had something in his hand, something small and flat."

We talk until I realize she knows nothing more to tell me, then I thank her and limp into town. I feel nothing. How do you feel things, Simon?

I show his picture to every shopkeeper, every passing pedestrian. Everyone shakes their head.

I change into my clean clothes at a service station, wash with paper towels, comb my hair, brush my teeth. This is important. I take my dirty clothes to wash at a laundromat, and as they're washing, I eat lunch in a diner. The waitress notices my bare feet but chooses not to fuss. I have a turkey sandwich, a Coke, two pieces of apple pie, and seven glasses of water. My legs throb and tingle and stiffen up, and I find it hard to stand again. The linoleum floor of the diner burns my wounded feet with its coolness. I can't walk anymore. I take wincing baby steps to the cash register. I never should have stopped.

I stay over one night in a bargain motel. In the morning I lever out of bed and crawl to the shower, standing in the warm water until a wash of diluted blood puddles under my feet and swirls down the drain. I comb my wet hair and touch the black scar of my chin.

I can barely walk.

I roll my belongings into my sleeping bag and head out of town anyway. As soon as I do, I can't feel him anymore, though I know he went this way. East. Due east. Sunset at his back, sunrise in his face. But I can't feel him. And in losing him, I lose myself.

I try to move my legs, but my steps remain short and jerky, like an old woman hunched over a walker. A little cry of pain accompanies each step, but this is the least of my worries.

The tunnel slams in, full and extensive, so long that no light filters along its length to meet me.

Somewhere in this siege I lose several days. I suppose, looking back, that they are days well lost.

I remember finding a creek, drinking my fill, rolling in it to soak my clothes in its icy relief, a strike against the gathering heat. I remember a glimpse of light as I do, and traces of blood left on the rocks as I step in and out.

Other than that, there is no accounting. No Simon, no time.

Still, life gives us so many days, often more than we would have ordered. Perhaps this is my way to strike back.

THEN:

GRANDMA STERLING'S HOUSE looked scarier in person and in color. It was the first thing I saw when I woke up. Then I saw Simon, resting his head on the steering wheel, his eyes open, unblinking, staring at his feet.

"Hey, Simon, how many people live in there?"

"Just one, I think."

I wanted to ask Simon why only one person would live in a house clearly big enough for twelve, but he seemed busy in his own head. I stared out the window.

Grandma Sterling trained roses to climb trellises on the sides of her house. She trained ivy to climb the gazebo in the side yard. Every window was framed by open shutters, every blade of grass a uniform green.

"Simon? How come we're not going in?"

He lifted his head as if a great, invisible weight rested on the back of his neck. "Okay, let's go, then."

On the way up the walk I took in the weedless border gardens, the two floors of smudgeless windows, and I wondered, when a person does all this, do they have time left over for other things?

On the way up the walk my heart pounded too hard, a sensation I could feel in my chest and hear in my ears, and I wanted to ask Simon if that was what scared meant. I didn't. Maybe he thought I already knew, and I didn't want to complicate his thinking.

I walked so close behind him I almost stepped on his heels, and I remember thinking the sun must have gone behind clouds, turning the red and green and white world a little grayer. I didn't know yet what that meant.

Simon stopped at the door and I slammed into his back, accidentally pushing him forward to knock once with his forehead. He stepped back in a stupor, as though he'd planned nothing so radical as knocking, but it was too late.

A woman opened the door, a woman with gray hair done up in a deliberate style, her dress starched and white, an apron flecked with roses. She smiled at Simon, exposing a row of large, perfect teeth, each one seeming to perform its role with grace. I had to wonder why, with those teeth going for her, her smile wasn't beautiful, like Mrs. Hurley's, and why I knew I'd never play a game designed to make Grandma Sterling smile.

"Yes, may I help you children?"

Simon spoke up. "Mrs. Sterling?"

"Yes, young man. How may I help you?"

"I'm Simon. This is Ella."

"Simon who, dear?"

"Simon Ginsberg."

A cloud passed across her metallic blue eyes, like the cloud I blamed for blocking the sun, turning Grandma Sterling's face a little grayer.

"Yes, I see." She looked past Simon to our car, as if expecting a busload of Ginsbergs. Then she conceded that we had best come inside.

We followed her to the parlor, her steps a smooth glide that tossed her skirt about her calves. I walked behind Simon, clutching the back of his shirt, wishing to be invisible. The hall seemed miles long, like a forced march down death row. My vision darkened at the periphery, until I could only identify those objects directly in front of me. A knickknack shelf with pearly blue and white porcelain figures dancing a minuet. A grandfather clock with a swinging pendulum and great, brass-chained weights.

I wanted to ask god to absorb me into the floorboards, to make me disappear, but I owned no god as yet, being too young to merit his attentions. I knew that, if seen, I could only be seen as not fitting here. I was not a child who lived in a house with a grandfather clock. I was a child who had to wash her hands before she could touch one. I was not a child who would be trusted to dust the fine bric-a-brac, but the one who would break something special.

Grandma Sterling sat in a frail wicker chair and Simon and I perched lightly on the edge of a love seat, my hip bumping against his. I thought if I touched as little of the furniture as possible she might admire my futile efforts not to defile her environment.

DeeDee spoke first. She said, *oh, man, did I warn you.* She laughed at us.

"You look a lot like your mother, Simon."

Grandma Sterling's voice echoed down to me, like a voice that breaks through a veil of sleep. My stranger-grandmother was drifting farther away. Or I was.

She asked Simon what brought us, and if we traveled alone, and how we found the trip. She focused only on Simon, her smile store-bought, her voice crisp, a voice reserved for asking questions of strangers when the answers don't matter. She never looked at me or called me by name. I began to think I might really be invisible, and the more sure I became, the more light flowed into my peripheral vision.

Simon stood and tugged at my sleeve. I didn't dare ask what I had missed. I followed him bumping-close into the kitchen, a sprawling white room with bay windows and hanging plants, by far the brightest room in the house, yet the light appeared black to me. I can't explain it any better than that.

Grandma Sterling set three blue willow china bowls on the table in front of Simon, then a quart of handpacked vanilla ice cream and a scoop, and slipped away to boil water for tea.

"Simon, is it dark in here to you?"

Simon gave me a funny look and pressed a hand to my forehead. I told him I felt fine and sat with my chin on the table, watching him scoop ice cream. It was packed hard, and he applied more and more pressure until the scoop slipped and a curl of ice cream skidded loose, flew into the air and landed on Grandma Sterling's kitchen linoleum.

For the first time in my life, it seemed poor Simon was in over his head. He stared at the blob on the floor, his eyes frozen wide in terror. I looked around to see Grandma Sterling filling a kettle, her back to us, and did the only right, logical thing. I grabbed the scoop out of Simon's hand and bumped him out of the way.

I wondered if he'd ask me later why I did it. I had plenty of time to wonder. Time slowed to a crawl as Grandma Sterling blew lightly on the burner and adjusted the flame.

I knew that, when she turned around and saw what had happened, she couldn't possibly think less of me than she already did. But Simon had a chance. I could tell by the way she looked at him—like he was there. Like she had pictured her grandson looking something like him, blond and fair-skinned and handsome. Why ruin Simon's chance?

When she turned, her face fell. She stood for a moment, hands on hips, as if the whole situation was simply too much for her. Then she moistened a linen towel and wiped up the mess. As she straightened up, a wisp of gray curl fell onto her forehead, and she brushed it back into place, seeming anxious to make everything perfect again.

"I guess we should have left that to your brother Simon."

"Yes, ma'am. Sorry, ma'am."

We ate our ice cream and drank our tea in the most deafening, wearing silence. It seemed to stretch forever, like the god mesa, only not beautiful in any way.

I glanced obsessively over at Simon, hoping he'd say it was time to go.

Grandma Sterling broke the silence. "Before you go, maybe you'd like to see the room where your mother grew up."

We followed her up carpeted stairs to the second floor, where she opened the door to my mother's bedroom and motioned us inside. She did not cross that threshold herself.

Then she disappeared, leaving us alone in a new world of retrospect. Simon breathed deeply when she left, as though he'd never breathed before.

"DeeDee thinks this is all pretty funny," he said.

"Well, she did warn us. Hey, Simon, is it supposed to be so dark in here?"

Simon held my face and stared into my eyes as though he might see some obvious evidence of my breakdown in vision.

"You okay, Ella?"

"Yeah, but we can't stay here, Simon. Not even if she said we could, and she won't."

"I know. Hey, look at this." He rolled his neck around as if to stretch out kinks. "Have you ever seen anything so clean? There's no dust in here. You think she dusts in here every day?"

I walked the walls of the room, staring at close range like an old blind woman. I saw a teenage girl's shelf of books, a bed with a ruffled spread, a locked diary on the nightstand. On the dresser I peered at a snow globe with Heidi inside, and a picture of my mother at about Simon's age, which I held in my hands.

"Wow, look at this, Simon. She was so beautiful." I felt his comforting presence at my shoulder. "I never saw her look this pretty. Did you?" Her hair clung to her skull in tight ringlets, her dark lashes curled like a doll's from her blue eyes. She wore a tight polka-dot dress.

"Yeah, a while ago, maybe. When you were little. She'd get all dolled up and Dad would take her dancing."

Something moved inside me. I knew then why my father fell in love with her, which had always been hard to fathom, watching her vegetate on the couch in her old housedresses, and curlers that never seemed to turn into a hairdo.

And then, knowing why someone would love her, I worried that she might not be okay.

"Where do you think she is, Simon? Do you think she's happy?"

Simon wouldn't, or couldn't, answer.

Just then Grandma Sterling appeared in the doorway, startling me, and the framed photo sailed out of my hands and landed on the braided rug. I rushed to redeem myself by picking it up, and kicked it out of my reach.

Grandma Sterling scooped it up and returned it to its rightful place on the dresser.

Simon grabbed hold of my wrist and pulled me downstairs and out the front door.

"Simon, dear," she called out as we trotted down her front steps.

Simon whirled as if sensing a gun held to his back. "Thank you for the ice cream, Grandma Sterling, but we can't stay."

"Before you go, dear . . ."

This is it, I thought. She'll say some little nice thing, now that she knows we're not staying long. Pleased to meet you. Come again. At least, tell my daughter I love her, which we could not have done. "Did your mother die?"

Later I would learn to guard against hope, but this one last time I had let a flagging sense of trust in the rightness of things pull me in.

My brother Simon only said, "What?"

"Did your mother die that time?"

"Uh, no. No, ma'am, she didn't."

"Oh. I just wondered."

Then the click of her door, no kinder than its owner.

"Why did she say that, Simon?"

"I don't know. Maybe the cancer surgery. Or because Dad tried to call."

"Oh, yeah."

We sat in the car together, and Simon leaned on the steering wheel and cried.

"We could go to Mrs. Hurley's," I said.

"We hardly know her."

"But she said if we were ever in Columbus we had to come see her. We can be in Columbus just as easy as Reading."

"I think she meant like in a year or two."

"But she didn't say in a year or two. Don't cry, Simon. I think Grandma Sterling liked you."

Simon laughed bitterly, but not as loud as DeeDee.

THE MOON DOESN'T SAY

SOMETHING PROPELS ME upward through a thick crust of uncon-
sciousness, cracking the surface to allow a scrap of light to bleed
through. A hand, behind my neck, a touch of warm metal at my
lips, then cool water. I try to take it in, gurgle and cough, spill it
down my chin and neck, but even there it is appreciated.

Now I lose another couple of days.

When I get one back again, it's fairly useless to me. I'm lying
on a couch in a modest cabin, in a long, clean white shirt, with a
sheet thrown over me. A noisy swamp cooler works against odds
to keep the air livable. The room is decorated in bones. Cattle,
coyote, rabbit, god only knows what. Feathers. Native American
pottery.

My feet lie propped and bandaged. They feel too heavy. I don't
move them, so I won't have to know what I've done.

My first visitor is about three years old, a towhead, with a baby
bottle of something amber, juice maybe, dangling from his
mouth. He runs up to the couch surrounded by hound dogs
whose whole bodies wag with the action of their tails.

I hear a sucking sound as he pulls the bottle free, and a squeak
of air rushing into the flattened nipple.

He seems startled to see me look back.

"Are you dead?" he asks.

"Apparently not."

"Mom said you might be dead."

"Looks like it got better."

"Right," he says, and runs away, the dogs running with him.

I decide on a little nap; or rather, it decides on me.

When I wake up, a woman sits on the edge of the couch with me. Kathy, so she says. Her golden-brown hair is gathered up onto her head, with just the right amount falling away again. She is younger than me. She hands me a cup that I assume contains water, but it's warm chicken broth. I drink it all at once and feel better.

"Thank you. How did I get here?"

"You walked. Rick found you in the front yard. You were delirious with fever. You probably don't remember."

I don't, but it doesn't seem necessary to say I don't. I'm sure the blankness on my face says it all. She is a stranger to me, yet I'm an old friend of the family by now. I've been with them for days.

She sits with me for a while, which I like, though I can't seem to say so, and tells me my fever was a hundred and four when I arrived. She and Rick wrapped me in wet sheets, and the doctor came and shot me full of antibiotics. He said my feet were so infected that in another three or four days he might not have been able to save them.

I try to thank her for finding me in time to save my feet. I can't very well follow Simon without them. She says I found her. Whatever. I want to ask how Simon's feet are holding up, and who will find Simon in time to save them, but I think she has enough trouble just saving me, so I ask where we are.

She says we're on the edge of Death Valley, fifteen miles from the nearest town.

I say I have money, I'll pay her back for the doctor, and she says we'll work that out when I'm better, that I should get some sleep, and in the process of doing so, I lose another day or two.

Long before my feet are ready to bear me, I decide to test the water, and I hobble out back to sit with Rick, my host, on rickety lawn chairs in the cool desert night. As soon as I take my first step I know it's a mistake, but I finish the job anyway.

"Mighta been too soon," he says, pointing to the clean dressing soaking through with blood.

"Guess so," I say.

He's a bearded young man, twenty-five maybe, with thin brown hair cascading down the back of his collar, and an easy smile, which he gives away for free. We sit silent for a while, not so much out of awkwardness as respect. A yellow hunter's moon hangs gigantic over a nearby mountain, washing the barrel cactus and prickly pears in a pearly, translucent light. Somewhere in the distance coyotes yip and bark in shrill voices, and the dogs' hackles rise.

I roll up my sleeves two turns, which I normally would not do, because he and his wife have seen the scars anyway.

"You know," Rick says, "you really can't walk across Death Valley barefoot. Or just about any other way. Temperature can get up to one thirty-five by day. You wouldn't make it, even starting out in good shape. You couldn't carry that much water."

"I'll be out of your hair as soon as I can," I say.

"You're not bothering us any. Stay till you're ready to move on. But let me drive you to Vegas. You can get a bus from there, hitchhike, whatever you need to do."

"If you'll let me buy the gas."

"It's not that far," he says. He tells me a few old Death Valley ghost stories. Predictable ones, punctuated by yawns. Then he excuses himself and goes in for the night.

I don't bother to tell him that I damaged my feet so badly walking out here, I wouldn't dare walk in again. I'd rather spend the night out in real life, anyway.

I gaze up at the man in the moon and wonder if Simon tried to walk across Death Valley. I wonder if anybody found Simon, put a hand behind his neck and poured water into his mouth. But the moon doesn't say what it knows.

Its light floods my eyes, bigger than life, and I realize the tunnel is gone completely, and I cry. Because Simon would be so proud if he were here, that I came through so well. Then I realize he'd be proud of me for crying, and I cry harder.

How do you stop crying, Simon?

THEN:

MRS. HURLEY DIED in Las Vegas, a little over a year after Simon and I found her again. We were there. The trip was an eighty-seventh birthday present, her own special request. The night before she passed away, she gave us an enormous handful of money that she'd won at the crap tables.

She said it was because she never would have won it without Simon to blow on her dice. I think she knew she'd have no need of it where she was going, and although she seemed ready enough to move on, it must have troubled her to leave us to our own devices.

The last thing she said to me was this: "Take care of that brother of yours." My mouth fell open. Simon needed no care that I could see, and surely I'm no caregiver. Her voice fell a little thin then, but I heard her loud and clear, though it took me a while to sort out what I heard. "I always worry about the ones say everything's okay." I'm still not sure I completely understand.

Simon tried to give the money back to Mrs. Hurley's daughter when she flew out to make the arrangements, but she wouldn't hear of it.

"If she gave it to you," she said, "she wanted you to have it."

We drove back to Columbus for our things, and for the funeral. Simon swears I attended, but I remember nothing to this day.

I know I'm leaving out a chunk of history, the whole year we lived with Mrs. Hurley, but at this point in time I remembered not one day of it, so I feel it does not rightfully belong here.

We moved to L.A., where Simon got a job as a gardener. By then he'd had experience. Simon was a good gardener. Plants couldn't wait to grow for Simon. He inspired them.

Simon found us a furnished room to rent in a private house less than two miles from Griffith Park. He enrolled me in school but I rarely attended.

He dropped me at school every morning on his way to work, and from there I usually walked to a stable at the edge of the park and stood in a corral with the horses. They accepted me immediately. Unlike people, they don't judge much by your outsides. They knew I was one of them.

Problem was, when one of the employees came around to ask what I was doing there, I was pretty caught up in being a horse, and I spooked. I felt my eyes widen, showing white all the way around, as I pictured it, and I flew straight up and came down dancing. And the other horses, they followed my lead. I considered that a high compliment, that they would stampede on my say-so.

Nobody else seemed to like it.

The man—I think his name was Frank—hauled me out of there and asked who I belonged to, but by then I'd forgotten. By then I thought I belonged to the earth and the sky, and the sharp, pushing blades of grass that grew for me.

Simon came and found me in time, and from then on they'd call him to come get me. Since he couldn't be reached at work, and he didn't come home until six, and since it caused a great stampede to scare me in any way, I found plenty of time to pursue equine grace.

Standing in that paddock, shuffling in the green grass, the blue sky looked a mile wide, and I had to squint against the open brightness of the world. But as soon as Simon packed me in the car to go home, the world narrowed and drew in, going to gray at the edges.

By the time we got back to our room, I had to stand a foot away and squint into his face as he talked to me, to follow his lips. Sometimes my hearing went a little flat, too.

"We're taking you to a doctor," he said one day, and I eventually conceded, though I felt it might be cheaper and more direct to allow me to stand out with the horses.

Simon bought me a health insurance policy, which required physical exams, and he stood close to me and held my hand during the eye exam, and talked to me about horses, and the harmonica Mrs. Hurley had given him, that used to belong to her freeman grandfather, and the tattoo of the rose I saw on her left shoulder. I'd forgotten all that. He even made me laugh, reminding me what she'd said when I saw it. "Never really know somebody, do you, child?" with a high-pitched giggle she usually reserved for evenings after a few slugs of apricot brandy.

I was diagnosed as having twenty-twenty vision.

Then Simon waited awhile to take me to the doctor, so it wouldn't appear shady.

In the evenings Simon and I would walk up to Griffith Park Observatory, or drive up if it had been a long day. Simon liked to look down at the lights of the city, and up at the lights of the stars, preferably both on the same night. He said it gave him a sense of perspective, how everything is relative to everything else. He said it reminded him that the world was so much bigger than just the part we'd already lived.

We'd stand in line to look through the telescope, sometimes twice in one night, at Mars, or the moon, and the astronomer would tell us which craters we could see, or the name of a mountain range. I think he liked us.

Simon told him he wanted to be an astronomer, but I didn't know yet that he meant it. We'd stay after, when the viewing time was over, and Virgil—that was the astronomer's name—would show us pictures in his books of the planets.

Maybe he took a liking to us because Simon told him we were on our own, that he, Simon, was my legal guardian and worked as a gardener to support us both.

At first I thought I might have ruined things by telling Virgil what I thought about the man in the moon. I said I knew exactly how he felt, floating up there in space, the only life on his barren planet, seen by a billion people who never believed he was real. Virgil thought about it awhile, then told me that just about every human being on earth must have felt that way at one time or another.

Still, I think it was Virgil who talked Simon into taking me down to County Mental Health. Not in a mean way. I think Simon asked him what to do, and that was his best answer.

Two things might have happened to cause Simon to ask for that advice. The first was the test results. I had an eye exam, and a brain scan, neurological testing, the whole nine yards. I was fine. Textbook normal. That concerned him, I think, because he might have wanted them to find some simple, obvious condition that could be treated with a drug or whatever.

Then, upset by this news, he came to me one night and asked me to promise never to do what our sister DeeDee did.

"Sure, Simon," I said, "no problem." I was always glad to do anything to help Simon out. "What did she do?"

About two weeks later he got me an appointment at Mental Health. He took the day off work to wait in the big, bare outer office with me, stiff on folding metal chairs, staring down at our feet and the checkered linoleum.

"Look," he said, "they're going to let you talk to a lady. Her name is Miss Rose. I want you to tell her everything that might help. Anything you can think of that's important."

"Okay, sure, Simon. How do I know what's important?"

"Well, just whatever bothers you, or what goes through your head. Just be real honest with her, okay? So she can help you."

Miss Rose wore a gray suit with a straight skirt, and a little teddy bear pin on her lapel. Her hair was thick and wild, like mine, only drawn back in a barrette and not given its freedom.

Her face was kind, but worn down.

She led me into a room with a narrow table and two metal folding chairs. I wasn't afraid, as far as I could tell.

"My name is Wilhelmina," she said, "but call me Willie. I like it much better. I hate the name Wilhelmina. What about you? Do you like the name Ella?"

I shrugged with genuine curiosity. I watched her face, looking for things to like about her, and doing well so far. "I never really thought about it. I mean, it's my name, right? Like it or not."

"How old are you, Ella?" I knew that Simon had told the lady at the desk, who had written it down on the same chart Willie held on her lap, so I concluded that she was attempting to put me at ease, which I already was. I debated how long I should humor her.

"I'll be thirteen next month."

"Your brother Simon brought you here, I see. Was it his idea, or yours?"

"Well, he thought of it, but I don't mind."

"Good," she said. "That's important."

My eyes drifted out her window to a solid wall of ivy that I knew in my head was a freeway embankment, but which I found strangely beautiful in that contrast, that frame. I'd been focusing strongly on green since my days in pasture seeing through the eyes of a horse. Just gazing out the window brought light into my field of vision.

"May I say some things?" I said. I knew it might take a while her way, and I wanted to tell her everything Simon would want me to say.

"Yes, of course, Ella—you can say anything you like."

"I can think of three things." I decided that sitting on a metal chair with my hands on my knees felt confining. "Can I sit on the windowsill?"

"Wherever you're comfortable, Ella."

From my window seat perch, if I looked up, I could see the cars on the freeway, feel the rumble of the big rigs rolling by, but I didn't mind any of that.

"Here's one, Willie. Have you ever met somebody—I'm just learning about this—who thinks they were born the wrong sex?"

"Yes, I have. Does that feel like you, Ella?"

"I don't think so. But have you ever met anybody who thinks they were born the wrong species?"

I didn't watch her face, so I'm not sure how any of this affected her. I fixed on green, my visual lifeline.

"Well, I'm not sure. Can you tell me any more about it?"

"I think god made a mistake with me. I think I should have been a horse. He probably has a lot on his mind, you know. I don't just mean I want to be a horse, or I wish I was. I mean I think I am, only stuck in the wrong shell."

"You think and talk well, Ella. I can tell you have a person's brain."

"Yes," I said. "That's the very most tragic part of the whole thing. Here's something else I need to tell. I feel all the time like I'm standing on something about the size of a toothpick. Over a deep well. A well with no bottom. And every single minute of every day, it's all I can do to stay up. It's a full-time job. Believe me, I get plenty tired. But what can I do?"

"Are you afraid of the well, Ella?"

"Oh, no. It's inviting. I'd love to just let go. What a relief that would be. It doesn't hurt to fall, you know, only to land, and the well has no bottom."

"So what do you think keeps you on the toothpick, then, Ella? If it's something you want to talk about at all."

"Oh, that's easy. Simon. He's lost everybody else to the well. It's important to him."

"You've told me quite a lot, Ella. I must say I'm surprised. You're very cooperative with me."

"Simon said to tell you what I could. Oh, one more thing. I saw something on the news last week. They're trying to pass a law that says dog pounds can't turn unwanted dogs over for lab experiments. The people who want them—you know, the experimenters—they say the dogs'll just die anyway. But you know why they want to pass the law? They say it's cruel to hurt them once they've known a decent home. They say it's not the same as a rat that's never known a better life, only pain."

"I can see that means something to you, Ella."

I turned my face in to Willie, away from the green, and watched my field of vision zoom into a spyglass pattern, darken to almost obscure her.

"Sometimes," I said, "I think it would be better if we'd never gone to live with Mrs. Hurley."

"Mrs. Hurley? Who was that?"

I said I didn't remember, and unfortunately, that was true.

THE SURFACE OF THE MOON

I SIT BACK against a Hopi blanket on the seat of Rick's truck, my shirt soaked through with sweat. I wipe it out of my eyes, and it tickles as it rolls into my collar. Across the hood of the old Chevy pickup, heat rises in waves, a shimmering disturbance to the natural order of the air. I lift my hat, wipe my forehead on my sleeve, and tuck it back down again.

I wiggle my toes in my heavy hiking boots, testing my level of pain. It's too soon, of course, but here I go.

Rick gave me the hiking boots. They're three sizes too big. "Just the point," he said, and supplied the accompanying five pairs of socks. "This way when your feet swell, and they will, you can peel off socks."

I thanked him and settled up my doctor and pharmaceutical bills, leaving me with fifty-three dollars' life savings. "You sure you're not cutting yourself too short," Kathy had said, at least four times.

"I'll do fine."

Of course I was cutting myself short. But Simon taught me to face financial needs as they arise. Never short current obligations for those you can't even see yet. That's what he used to say.

Vegas is a dream on the unseen horizon. I've been there twice before. Once saying hello to Mrs. Hurley, once saying goodbye. For the longest time I hated hellos, thinking the one leads to the other.

Rick always says what's on his mind. I tolerate this in him because he saved my life and then some, but it's a character trait that tends to make me want to fly away.

"You know," he says, "if your brother tried to walk through here—"

"Rick," I say. I don't need to elaborate. He nods and falls silent. I must have mentioned Simon in my delirious moments. Since coming to my senses, I haven't said his name aloud once—an attempt to circumvent this moment.

I think of the bleached bones on Rick's walls and mantel. Then I don't anymore.

He stops at the Las Vegas bus station. I reach across the seat to shake his hand. It's a strong grasp, on both of our parts, full of respect, and the regret of parting.

"Thanks for everything," I say, and he shifts his eyes to the floor and shakes his head. Gratitude and charity must have muddled in his brain. He won't take it.

I tell him to thank his wife again, and that I hope his kid grows up strong and safe.

I step down to the pavement and disguise my initial wince of pain by waving to the tailgate of Rick's retreating Chevy.

A bus station clerk with an untrimmed mustache and visible undershirt lines says the next bus east won't leave for over an hour. I buy a ticket to Gallup, the farthest I can afford to go. My change amounts to fourteen dollars.

I ease my way down the street to the Starlight Casino. I'm testing two theories at once. I might be able to walk, get on a roll with it, put the pain aside. And I might be willing to think about her now, with all these years to buffer me.

The walking is a bust. I figure I'll be lucky to make it back to the bus station. The Mrs. Hurley part goes somewhat better.

I limp into the casino and find the crap tables, thinking I will locate the very one. But everything changes with the seasons. The whole layout feels wrong.

I know I am out of place, a rugged desert wanderer, a prospector, one step removed from the earth. I don't mind. Wherever I go, I know I am out of place.

I can see her, although I understand that she's just a waking dream, shaking the dice in a loose fist in the air, then holding them out for Simon to blow on. The crowd loved her. Eighty-seven years old, and on her last roll ever. The one that would have to do for eternity.

I had to tell her when it was over, and she lost almost a thousand back, wishing I'd be wrong. The crowd was with her. *No, no, let her play.* But Simon knew, too, and wouldn't blow on the dice. We weren't trying to ruin her moment, we just knew it was over.

"What you mean, child? I'm winning."

But then she threw a two. Later she thanked us. It's always easier to spot the end of somebody else's roll.

I hobble back to the bus station, and it feels like all the walking I can handle for the month. When I climb on the bus, I take a good look at the driver and decide he's about fifty. Maybe he was working this route twenty-five years ago, I think. Maybe he put Mrs. Hurley off the bus.

But then I think, even if he did, which is not likely, what would I feel about that? I suppose I would have to thank him.

Something nags me about the ancient car trip to Las Vegas and back. There with Mrs. Hurley, back without her. Something Simon saw, or liked, or both, but I can't reach it. It plays games with me, slipping away if I grab too hard.

I should have walked, I think. I'll lose the trail. But of course, I lost the trail many miles ago, though I only just now admit it. Even the hawk is gone.

The desert rolls by the window in darkness, like the surface of the moon.

THEN:

ON MY FOURTH appointment with Willie, I saw a poster tacked to the bare walls of the room with different-colored push pins. A band of wild horses, galloping across a plain, throwing dirt in clouds under their hooves, coats wet, muscles long and traceable. I smiled, watched her face in the remainder of my peripheral vision. Watched her light up to match me.

Then, without warning, I shut down. I sank into the hard metal chair, turned my face to the window, staring into blankness.

"What's wrong, Ella? Do you want me to take it down?"

I looked up at the poster again, deciding.

"They're going to go off without me. My legs aren't long enough. I'll never catch up."

She stood and began removing push pins, but I stopped her.

"No, don't. If you take it down, they'll be gone."

That was the session I introduced Willie to my sister DeeDee. They got along swimmingly, I thought, and both seemed polite to each other, but then Willie suggested we up our sessions to three times a week.

I didn't mind.

A few weeks later Simon called Uncle Manny. He did that now and then, every two or three months, to report our continued status as live humans. That's how Simon found out our father had been released.

We stood squeezed into the same phone booth on Griffith Park Boulevard, cars and buses droning past, pairs and groups of restless youth out walking for its own sake. While Simon dialed the number I watched a scared coyote dodge through lane after lane of traffic, then skitter out of the street and leap over a residential fence.

I tried to focus on these things as Simon called our father. I heard him say, "Yeah, well, I called Manny. What else was I supposed to do? I didn't know how to—"

Then my hearing scoped down to near nothing, receptive only to the deep base of engine noise, and the night grew darker, like the blackness of a tunnel, or a well, broken only by the headlights of passing cars, illuminating nothing.

"He wants us to come see him," Simon told me, shaking me gently by the shoulders to bring me back.

"So are we going?"

"Well, if you feel up to it, it would be nice. He offered us some money. We need it. The money Mrs. Hurley gave us is almost gone."

We set off on foot down the boulevard toward home.

I thought that money would last forever.

We left after school the following day—or rather, after what would have been school, if I'd bothered to go. Simon took part of the afternoon off from work. We arrived in the early evening.

The corner of the roof was still scorched. Thick tufts of grass pushed up through cracks in the concrete slab that had once formed our garage floor. I stared up into the late sun, taking in the attic windows that Simon and I had scaled at night, and the sky blackened and faded, leaving me smaller in its dark wake.

I stepped in the door; the house felt close and heavy, infectious almost, as if sickness lived inside, waiting to attack the unsuspecting with every breath. My vision narrowed to a pinprick of light, and I held my arms out in front of me for radar and balance, and bounced off furniture anyway.

I never saw my father.

I heard him say, "What is this with Ella—why can't she see?"

"She's fine, Dad. She's been to doctors. She's okay."

"Oh, yeah? Well, if she's so okay, why can't she see where she's going?"

He took hold of me then, grabbed me by both of my bare wrists, and I screamed and twisted away from him and ran out the back door, slamming into walls and door frames and spinning away again. I caught a glimpse of dusky sky as I shot across the back yard for the fence, and I heard my brother Simon say, "She's going to counseling. Why can't you just leave her alone?"

I scaled the back fence and felt my way into the three-acre woodlot, knowing there was something in there I didn't like, but not knowing what it was, or how it could be worse than the house behind me.

My field of vision opened like a sea urchin bubbling outward, searching. I sat in the dirt with my back against a tree, before remembering I didn't like trees. My wrists felt hot and itchy where he touched me.

I heard Simon a couple hundred yards away, calling my name, fading off in the wrong direction. That's when I saw it, lying in the dirt, a yard or so off my left foot. A bright yellow disposable lighter. I figured it must be out of fluid—otherwise why would someone throw it away?—but it worked fine.

Do it, DeeDee said, *now. Quick. Before it's too late. Remember the dog.*

I adjusted the flame all the way out, like a blowtorch, and arrested the disease before it could spread down into my hands, up my arms, take me over and own me. It didn't hurt.

I'd never seen Simon so upset.

"Ella, my god, no!"

He tackled me out onto the leafy dirt and wrestled the lighter away, all of which seemed like unnecessary histrionics to me. If he had just told me another way to keep safe, I'd have gladly put the lighter back where I found it.

"Ella, don't you get it? You can't do things like this. You can't." He sounded so brave and grown up while his eyes welled up with tears and spilled over. "Why do you think Willie lets you stay at home? Because I told her you never hurt yourself and nobody ever hurts you."

I touched his face.

"Don't cry, Simon. If it really bothers you, I won't do it again."

Then we heard our father's voice, calling after us, and Simon threw me over his shoulder and we ran around the long way, through the gap in the fence, out the side street, and to our car.

Before we could drive away, our father stood in front of our bumper, blocking the way, reaching into his pocket for his wallet. Simon tried to pull around him but he blocked us off again and signaled that he only wanted to give us some money.

"Cover your wrists," Simon hissed at me, and I crossed them behind my back. It hurt.

"Here," my father said through the window, his face thick and sad through the forced darkness. "You'll need this." He slipped Simon a wad of bills. "You need more, you call your Uncle Manny. I'll give him some money to get to you if you need it. Anything you need. Don't you think I worry about you? Do you know how it feels not to know where your own kids are?"

Simon threw the Studebaker into drive and left him in our figurative dust.

I didn't imagine it could be any worse than not knowing where your own mother is.

Simon took me to the emergency room, where they asked a lot of questions. I said I was playing with matches, and the fire got out of hand, and I burned myself trying to put it out.

They bandaged my wrists and wrote a prescription for antibiotics, and something Simon could give me later for the pain, so I could sleep. They said I'd have to see a doctor again in a few days. Maybe even get skin grafts. But they let me go home.

Simon called Willie and said I was sick, which might have made her a little bit suspicious, because she called me at home while Simon was at work during the day.

I said I would come in next week when I felt better and tell her all about it, even though Simon said I shouldn't, because Simon didn't know I could tell her a lot of things he wouldn't, because he doesn't know her, and because he worries too much. I promised that nobody had hurt me in any way, and that everything would remain in control until then. She gave me her number at home and said I could call any time, if I was in trouble, or needed to talk.

When I saw her the next week, I wore long sleeves, like Simon told me to, but when I got alone inside her room, with the galloping horses, I rolled up my sleeves and let her see my bandages.

"Simon is scared you'll make me go away if I hurt myself. But what if I just made a mistake once? You'd trust me not to do it again, wouldn't you?"

Willie's eyes seemed to take back the heaviness they'd lost in my presence. "If you could tell me what happened and why, and I knew you really understood, I'd believe you. Unless it kept happening."

I told her the story of the dog DeeDee and I found over by the railroad tracks, years ago. A stray German shepherd with almost no hair. His skin was red and swollen, weeping. It hurt to look at him. We thought he'd been burned in a fire. He followed us for a while, and sat with us by the bus bench, but a man waiting for the bus told us not to touch him. He said the dog had the mange, which was a little parasite that gets under his skin, and pretty soon it just takes over the whole dog. He said if we touched him, it would get under our skin, too.

She watched my eyes during this story, but she knew me well enough by then; she didn't interrupt. She knew I'd make my point in my own good time.

"Simon took me to see our father. He's back."

"Back from where, Ella?"

"Where? Oh. You know, Willie, I can't remember. Anyway, I didn't want him to touch me, but he touched my wrists. I thought if I didn't kill the sickness right there, it would take all of me over. I promised Simon I'd never do it again."

"Do you understand why that's important, Ella?"

I gazed off through the window to green ivy. I didn't look at the horses, because I wasn't sure what they'd think of me just then. They'd probably think it's my human brain, and feel lucky themselves.

"No, Willie, I don't. But a promise is a promise. Besides, we're not going to go visit him anymore."

"Simon's right that this is serious, Ella. But if you keep coming in three times a week, and nothing like this happens again, I'm willing to trust you."

I wondered how old Willie was. Sometimes, like when I first saw the galloping horses, she looked about thirty. Now her eyes made me think she might be fifty or more. I wondered if I'd let her down in some way I didn't understand.

"You know, Willie, I never meant to hurt myself. I just didn't want the disease. I wouldn't do something against me. I don't think anybody ever does. You must know that, Willie. Everybody's just trying to stay safe. Even people who try to kill themselves, I bet they're still on their own sides, Willie. They just want to kill the pain. Everybody just wants to kill the pain."

Willie sat with her elbow on the table, her hand shading her eyes.

"I wish you knew how remarkable you are, Ella. So much deeper than anybody else I know. Even the grownups."

"Is that good, Willie? To be deep?"

She took her hand down and her eyes looked moist.

"Well, it is and it isn't," she said, "when you're trying to kill the pain."

I thought about a well with no bottom, but I didn't let go.

I touched Willie's face and told her not to cry, that everything would be okay.

SIMON'S MESA

THROUGH MOST OF the night, through most of Arizona, I sit awake, face pressed against the cool window, feeling my feet swell. Every mile looks like every other in this light, unless my vision pulls out to the horizon. This, though, I have found to be true on any terrain, in any sense. The shorter your range of vision, the fewer options and changes to trouble you.

Near the eastern border, near the end of my bus trip, I slide into a murky sleep, and even as I drift, it teases me. Something about our trips across Arizona, Simon's and Mrs. Hurley's and mine. Or rather, somewhere about it.

I jump awake, a second or an hour later, the question still playing in my mind, the answer stretched before me, waiting for me to open my eyes.

The sky streaks with light, and the edge of a ball of morning fire touches the eastern corner of an endless mesa. Simon's mesa. I try to swallow, but nothing happens. It's the answer to my question, so I might not want it. I might need it to go away.

I know now that Simon found his way back to that mesa, unless he couldn't. He is there or he is nowhere at all.

My legs feel hollow, my feet detached, the property of someone else entirely. If I sit frozen much longer, it will be too late. At sixty-five miles per hour, even the endless mesa will fade into history.

A heavy older woman sleeps beside me. She does not wake up when I push past her legs.

My feet scream complaints at me, which is to say they concede my ownership. I walk up the silent aisle to the driver. I speak quietly, because he and I are the only ones awake.

"I see I'm not supposed to talk to you when the bus is in motion. But this is important." I point to Simon's mesa, which he could hardly miss, as it forms the entire north horizon. "I need to get up there. Is there a road?"

His voice sounds gravelly, I'm guessing from coffee, cigarettes and lack of practice. "Up here three miles or so, there's a route— I forget the number. It goes due north. I don't suppose it takes you all the way up to that mesa, but it goes as far as any pavement goes in that direction. That's Indian country. Navajo and Hopi reservation."

"Then I need to get off up there."

"Sorry," he says, his voice oiled now with use, "no can do. I have to let you off at a regular stop."

Right, I think, *tell it to Mrs. Hurley.* "What if I was causing all sorts of problems? Cussing you out, waking up the passengers. Then wouldn't you have to put me out wherever it happened?"

He shoots me a helpless, exhausted look. "You wouldn't do that, though, would you?"

"Not if I didn't have to."

I fetch my bedroll from the overhead rack. He pumps the brakes slowly, quietly, and eases the bus to a stop on the shoulder. I give a little salute as I limp away.

The sun is out of hiding, weak across Simon's mesa but threatening big things. Telling me, *wait, just wait. I'll have my say.*

I hobble along the center line of a straight ribbon of pavement, free of cars, people, animals. Free of everything but roller-coaster dips and me.

I argue with my madness. Because, you see, if it would come back now, this pain would mean nothing to me. I could walk for days. It wouldn't matter that I'd brought no food again, or that the sun sapped my moisture and I carried no replacement. It wouldn't even matter that I'd likely left Simon's bleached bones a whole state behind me.

I need it badly now, the madness. Just a few days ago it came running when I called it, but now it only laughs at me. It reminds me of the years I referred to it as a stray cat and refused to feed it, knowing it would eventually move to more fertile ground. It says that if I were to ask a dog or a horse to come to me and stay, I'd have to put down proper bedding, a tub of water, a feeder, shelter. Without these basics, my guests would wither and die. But they have no choice, my madness insists, whereas it does. It tells me to have fun on my own.

On my own, every step is a torment, the sun a threat, the night which will follow it a threat. Without it I see Simon's mesa in one direction, food and water in the other.

I ask DeeDee what to do. She says nothing. Not because she chooses not to talk, but because there is no DeeDee. Not as such. I even experiment with the possibility that she might be dead.

I sit by the side of the road, leaning back on my bedroll, gauging the distance to that horizon. Fifteen miles? A hundred?

I hear the drone of a motor, and I stick my thumb out over the roadway. I see an old International Harvester pickup truck, driven by a man with a broad, dark face. The seat beside him is stacked with birds in wire cages.

He pulls onto the shoulder, and I try to run to meet him, but I can't run, and I'm afraid he will leave again before I can get there. He watches me in the rearview mirror, comfortable in his own patience. I scramble up onto the truck bed, and feel the tires skid on the gravel beneath me, the air move inside my clothes. I lean my head on my bedroll, watch the sky fade, not to tunnel vision, but in surrender to sleep.

THEN:

SIMON ACCEPTED A dinner invitation from Virgil and his wife Ruth for two days before I was to check into the hospital for my skin grafts.

I was in a far corner of the Griffith Park Observatory, after the telescope room had technically closed to the public, staring at the astronomy charts on the walls. Maybe they thought I couldn't hear. I listened so poorly by then, I think it was easy to fall into a habit of talking right in front of me.

"It might be a bad time for Ella," Simon told him. "She still has to be on pain pills, and with this hospital stuff coming up—"

"Actually," Virgil said, "that's why I suggested it. I thought she might be worried or nervous, and the break in routine might do her good. But it's totally up to you."

"I'll ask her."

Simon asked on the drive home if I cared to go. He said Virgil lived way out in the Antelope Valley, where you can see the stars better, without all the city lights, and he had his own observatory built on next to the garage.

"Simon, does Virgil like me?"

"Of course he does, Ella. Why would you ask that?"

"Do you think his wife will like me?"

"Well, sure—what's not to like?"

I only shrugged. I'd been noting that people backed off when I talked to them, drew their energy in like housewives pulling their children off the street. I preferred not to express this in words.

"I guess we should go, then."

For the occasion, Simon bought me a dress. It made me nervous, though I didn't say so. It made me feel like I should be someone different for them. I wore it without comment.

We drove out on Saturday afternoon, watching the last remnants of the city die away, the earth become bare and untouched, the way I pictured the surface of the moon. It didn't surprise me one bit that Virgil would live out here.

"I thought this might be good for you," Simon told me. "For us. To be around real people. You know, normal people. Do you know Virgil and his wife have been married for forty-two years? They were high school sweethearts. That's the way you do it, Ella. Find one woman, somebody special, and just be with that one woman the rest of your life."

Suddenly the surface of the moon felt barren and forbidding.

"Is that what you'll do, Simon?"

"Well, not right away," he replied, as if he could talk over his awkward guilt and I, of all people, wouldn't hear it. "Later, when you're all grown up and you can take care of yourself. And even then, we don't have to live far apart. We'll live out in the country and I'll be an astronomer."

"Simon, can you be an astronomer without going to college?"

"No, I don't think so. I'll have to go to college."

"Later? When I'm grown up?"

"Yeah, that's right. When you can take care of yourself."

Against great odds, and with much conscious will, I tightened my mental grip on that toothpick.

Virgil's house was a sprawl of stucco and red tile roof on four acres of ranch land. I knew it was his, even off in the distance, by the domed roof of the observatory.

Virgil seemed looser and more natural at home. Ruth, a dark-haired woman with streaks of gray and a round face like Mrs. Santa Claus, made a great effort to show that she liked me, long before she'd seen enough of me to tell. That was a bad sign, I knew, almost as bad as deciding she didn't like me before I had a chance to show her the truth.

She served chicken and dumplings, and homemade peach shortcake, and asked if I went to school.

"Not as often as I should. Simon has a lot of long talks with me about that." I almost went on to tell her why, how the kids called me a loon, and made fun of me, and tripped me in the hall. But DeeDee, who stood just behind and to the left of me, kicked my chair and told me to shut up. "Sometimes I go to visit the other horses, and sometimes I walk down to the old folks' home to see Mrs. Hurley."

DeeDee snorted laughter. She said, *yeah, but she's never there, though.* DeeDee and I had a running argument about the woman we visited. She insisted it was not Mrs. Hurley, but I felt sure it was, even though she went by a different name. That was something Mrs. Hurley would do in a mischievous moment, or after a few belts of apricot brandy.

Simon looked uncomfortable. That's when it dawned on me, what it meant to spend time with real people. Normal people. It meant that everybody was real but me, and even my brother Simon fell on the other side of the fence, out of my reach.

I practiced silence.

After dinner Virgil showed us his observatory, and Simon helped him open out the dome. Virgil let him sift through his library and borrow any books he wanted.

He focused the telescope on the half moon, because we'd seen the moon most often in Griffith Park, and he wanted us to see the difference without the city lights.

Before I looked, I asked the most important question on my mind.

"Can DeeDee look, too?"

The room went quiet, then DeeDee broke the stillness, saying, *boy, you really blew it this time.*

"DeeDee?" Virgil said. I wondered if Simon had even told him who she was.

"Go on, DeeDee," I said, because I felt guilty that she never got to look—at the city observatory there was always a line, and it wouldn't seem right to hold it up for what might appear as a blank space.

DeeDee had bigger things on her mind. *What the hell do I want to see the sky for, jerk? I'd rather watch this fight brew.*

What fight? I asked her, careful not to say it out loud, because, although Simon and I never fought, he did seem concerned, and I knew I'd said more than enough already.

Look at his face, she said. *You really screwed up. Boy, wait till the ride home, kid. Man, is he gonna come apart all over you.*

"Shut up, DeeDee," I said, hearing too late that I'd not only said it out loud, but far too loud.

Simon said nothing on the first half of the ride home. I'd never seen him direct and measure his silence so carefully.

Then he broke the moon-stillness, making me jump.

"You know, Ella, when DeeDee died—"

"Simon, doesn't it seem funny to see the moon up there, and then look around and feel as though we're driving on it?"

"Stop that, Ella. You have to listen. At first it was okay, what we did. We weren't ready to let go yet. But we're both older now. It's just not a good game anymore."

I felt a sway in my balance, and tried to jump into the conversation, as though the motion of words could set me right again. No words came out. I tried to fall back on DeeDee for balance, but she came out from under me like a throw rug on a waxy floor.

He's right, jerk. Open your eyes. When I left, I left. Who do you think you're doing all this for, anyway?

"You know," I said, "we should have dessert more often. Fresh dessert, like with peaches, like we had tonight. All we ever eat are sandwiches." Simon shook his head. "Do I embarrass you, Simon?"

He didn't answer.

He went straight to bed when we got home, no bath or anything, and I changed into my regular clothes, my jeans and comfortable sweatshirt. I tried to lie down but I was falling. Falling fast. A terrifying, thrilling sensation, the way I pictured it might feel to jump out of a plane and drop hundreds of feet per second, my stomach unable to register the shock.

I slipped out of our room and stumbled to the corner of the street, willing my vision to open out, demanding it serve me. I found the phone booth, but the path closed again, a flower in the night shadows, and I felt for the last hole on the dial, called the operator, and asked her to dial Willie's number for me.

"Hi," I said. "It's me, Ella. Am I calling too late?"

"No, I told you, anytime you need to call. Is anything wrong?"

"Oh, no, everything's fine, Willie."

"You sure?"

"Yeah. Fine. Except I can't see, so I'm not sure how to walk home."

"Where are you, Ella?"

"On the corner by my house. Right by Vermont Avenue. Just south of Griffith Park Boulevard."

"Does Simon know where you are?"

"He's asleep."

"Okay, I'll be there in about fifteen minutes, Ella. Wait right there for me, okay?"

"Sure, Willie. Don't hurry. I'll be here."

After all, where could I go? It's not like the well had a bottom to hit, or any direction to go but down.

She picked me up and drove me to Norm's Restaurant on Sunset and Vermont, and drank coffee and bought me a hot chocolate, and asked me to tell her what had happened.

"What makes you say something happened?"

"Okay," she said. "Take your time."

My line of sight opened slightly, maybe because she was there to fill it, maybe because the hot chocolate warmed it into expanding. She looked tired and blank, so ready to be what I needed that she'd forgotten to bring herself along.

"Why do you like me so much, Willie?"

She poured cream into her coffee and rubbed her eyes.

"In my job," she said, "I talk to people day after day after day. I've been doing it for twenty years. Most of them never tell me what goes on inside their head. It's like if you were an auto mechanic, and people brought their cars in for you to fix, and refused to open the hood."

"Simon only pays seven dollars a time for me to see you. That's not very much money for what you do."

"Well, it works on a sliding scale, Ella. If he had more, he'd pay more. Besides, he doesn't pay me. The county pays me. And it takes more from some and less from others."

"Do you get paid extra for seeing me tonight?"

"No, I don't."

"So you really just do this because you want to?"

"What happened, Ella?"

"Nothing. Nothing happened. Really. I'm more worried about what might have happened a long time ago, that I don't even know about yet, or what might happen later if I do too good a job of holding myself up."

"What do you mean, holding yourself up?"

"You know, like not falling into the well."

"What do you think will happen if you do too good a job?"

"I don't know. Can I get another hot chocolate?"

Much as I wanted Willie to like me, to greet her with the usual open hood, I'd grown wary of becoming the sort of person who could take care of herself.

WHAT ELSE BUT SPIRIT

WHEN I WAKE, the sky is still blue. Still wide. I'm still in the back of the pickup but the wheels are stationary, the engine quiet. My neck feels stiff, my hip pinched from its contact with corrugated steel.

I hear boot heels on wood planking. I raise my head to see that the truck is parked in front of a run-down, apparently defunct diner, and the driver who picked me up is walking out onto the front deck.

He stops at the edge of the last plank, squats down until his buttocks rest on his heels. Staring off into the distance, he begins to roll a cigarette.

His face is strong and dark, wide with years, and although it seems youthful, almost babyish, I sense the youth to be the lie in this dichotomy. His skin shows weather and wear, like saddle leather left too long in the wind and sun. He wears a deep, old scar across one eye. He is dressed much like I am. Jeans, a loose white shirt, heavy, thick-soled boots. Wide-brimmed hat. His hands are garnished with silver and turquoise, his nails bitten to the quick.

I raise up to a sit, and in doing so, catch his eye.

"This is the end of the line, I'm afraid. I didn't see any reason to wake you."

"Thank you for the ride," I say, and he dips his head in a gesture of assent. I ask if I may show him a picture of a man, in case he has seen this man go by. He dips his head again, and I pull Simon's picture from my bedroll and venture down.

The threat of the sun has been delivered. My feet are swollen with the day's heat, and my huge boots feel too small.

He notices my limping gait but says nothing.

I sit on the deck beside him, put the photo in his hand. He smokes with the other.

I gingerly pull off my boots and socks, and he watches without comment as I peel away the bloody bandages.

"I haven't seen this man."

"I see. Well, thank you. If I can just take a minute to change these dressings, I'll move along."

"You don't bother me by being here."

I pull fresh gauze from a paper bag stuffed into my bedroll. He watches the process in silence.

I say, "He might have been wearing only overalls."

"Your husband?"

"Husband? No. I have no husband."

"I'm sorry. I shouldn't jump to conclusions. I thought the man in the photo was your husband."

"No, he's my brother Simon."

I know he's thinking we look nothing alike, but he won't say so. He says only what is necessary, a quality I respect.

"Up the road another twenty miles or so, toward the long mesa, on this road, you'll find some shops. Not even a town, really, just a trading post, a feed store, and a hogan sort of a building where a man sells hunting rifles. The man's name is Sam Roanhorse. He's a friend of mine. We race pigeons together. About two months ago he told me a white man came into his shop and bought a rifle and ammunition. I don't think he would have thought much about it, other than it was a good cash sale, but the man wore only overalls. No shirt or shoes. And he came on foot and left on foot. Not in the direction of any civilization, either. North toward the mesa. Sam wondered what sort of a man would walk in this heat with no shirt. He said the man's shoulders were badly sunburned. Would your brother do a thing like that?"

I shake my head, words slow to cut through this flood channel of new information. It sounds like something I would do, but not my brother Simon.

"I don't know. But I'll find your friend Sam Roanhorse and show him the picture."

"Yes, do that, if it's important to you. And I know it must be, if you've come this far."

I don't know how far he thinks I've come, but I feel no tendency to argue. I will accept whatever he says he knows.

When my feet are bandaged and eased back into my boots, I hobble inside, with my host's permission, to drink water from his faucet. It will be several weeks, he says, until he can open as a restaurant. There is so much work to be done. He has only just purchased land, house, diner. The previous owner he classifies as a sloppy man.

No food yet, but he offers me a gift of the leftovers from his packed lunch, a round of fry bread, an apple and a pear.

"My wife always packs more than I can eat." Then he asks if I have a guide. "I think you must," he says, "or how could you sit on a porch with the very man who can tell you where to look next for your brother? I don't believe these things happen by accident. Do you know what I mean by a guide?"

"I'm not sure I do. No."

"Where I grew up, which is right here in the Navajo Nation, it would usually be an animal."

"Oh, you mean like a spirit guide."

"What else is there but spirit?"

After digesting this comment for a bit, I explain that I had a hawk, but he seems to have left me behind.

"Then he was not your guide. Or if he was, you left him behind."

"Maybe I found my way to you not by guidance, but by an ability within myself."

113

"Of course," he says. "All guidance springs from an ability within yourself—if only the ability to be guided."

He tells me his name is Everett Ankeah. He asks if I will join his wife and him for dinner later that evening.

"You should walk at night anyway. Midday, now, is the time to rest in the shade. Besides, she always cooks more than I can eat."

THEN:

SIMON CHECKED ME into the hospital on Monday morning for my skin grafts, and I worried that he missed too much time from work because of me.

He sat with me during all the visitors' hours, which only amounted to about four a day, and Willie came to see me both days on her way home from work, and brought flowers.

I left the hospital on Wednesday afternoon. I was supposed to stay in bed for three days, but I walked to the old folks' home to see my friend. I just called her my friend by then, tired of arguing with DeeDee over whether it was Mrs. Hurley or not.

I didn't take my pain pills because I didn't want to get foggy on the trip. I didn't mind the pain. It felt clean and functional. I brought Willie's flowers to give to my friend, who swore her name was Ruby McBride.

She looked an awful lot like Mrs. Hurley, I thought, the smile, the sense of humor, the grace, but DeeDee said her teeth were too straight, her face too full, and she didn't wear her hair in a braid. I took this to mean only that DeeDee had gotten in the habit of watching for details that carried no meaning.

I sat gingerly on the wooden chair by her bed, first pulling out a little slack in my loose sweatpants. They'd taken a piece of skin off the top of my thigh to transplant onto my wrists.

She sat up in bed, legs dangling over the side, and a beam of sun through the bare window lit up her face with its own special character. Round and friendly. A flicker of a thought said it might not be the exact same special character as Mrs. Hurley, if I could remember her.

I volunteered to massage Mrs. McBride's feet, something I used to do all the time for Mrs. Hurley. She used to call me an angel every time I did. She used to say the good Lord must not mind drinkers and gamblers, because he saw fit to send down two angels of her own, to make her last days luxurious.

"Won't it hurt your wrists though, love?"

"Oh, no, they don't hurt a bit." It was easier than explaining that pain had become an ally, and actually my thigh hurt a lot worse.

I pressed my thumbs along Mrs. McBride's instep, enjoying the look and feel of the shiny dark skin, so much like *hers*, although DeeDee and some part of me said that Mrs. Hurley's feet might have been a little bonier.

She asked me to tell her something about this Mrs. Hurley. I didn't answer. First because I didn't remember. Then because the pain wasn't welcome anymore, and I wanted to go home.

I ran most of the way.

When Simon got home he was angry.

"I had to take off work early to go see your principal. He wants to know what we're going to do, Ella. You're going to have to take your freshman year all over again, because now you're flunking the summer school that was supposed to get you through. I keep asking you about it, and you keep saying you'll go, and you never do."

"I wish you wouldn't be mad at me, Simon."

"How can I help it, Ella? I work so damn hard—"

Mrs. Hurley used to try to teach me to get mad. It was upsetting to her, how much help I needed. She'd never met anyone who couldn't do it naturally. She'd have me practice in front of a mirror, pretending to talk to someone like Grandma Sterling. "Repeat after me. *Just who in hell do you think you are?*" I parroted the words, but remained unclear on the concept, and watching her own anger rise didn't help.

Simon made salami sandwiches, then handed me a fresh peach he'd bought on the way home. We didn't talk while we ate.

After dinner we walked down to Hollywood Boulevard, to the appliance store. On the way I asked Simon to please not be mad at me.

"I'm not exactly mad, Ella. More like frustrated. Do you know what I'd give for a chance to go to school?"

At first it sounded like a good idea. *You go to school, I won't.* But the catch was there, obvious, too obvious to run through.

As long as he had to be the one to work, he said, he at least wanted to know that I was using that opportunity while I could.

"But I can't, Simon. I just can't."

We seemed predisposed to butt again and again into a built-in stalemate, because I couldn't say why not. I might almost have told Willie, but not Simon. I couldn't possibly bear to have Simon feel all that shame on my behalf.

We walked in silence past the Hollywood apartment houses, with their green lights trained onto palm trees and motel-like railed outdoor stairs.

A crowd was gathered on the street in front of the appliance store. Simon had to hoist me onto his back so I could see. Most of our fellow onlookers were bums and winos, bag ladies and prostitutes. Everybody else had their own TV at home.

I watched the surface of the moon on the seven displayed television screens, and wondered why I liked it better through Virgil's telescopes. Then it hit me. It wasn't supposed to have some clown in a space suit bouncing around on it.

It was ruined.

"Why'd they take it away from us, Simon?"

"Take what away?"

"The moon."

"They didn't. They just stuck an American flag in it, and now they'll pick up some rocks and stuff."

"That's what I mean."

I looked up at the man in the moon and wondered if he felt the way people in the newspaper say they feel when their houses have been burglarized, or when they've been molested. I knew I did. It melted into a heavy feeling in my stomach, a depression that pulled me down closer to the sidewalk. I wondered if I felt any heavier to Simon.

When the coverage turned mostly to repetition, and I threatened to fall asleep on Simon's back, he let me down and we walked home.

"Think we'll ever get it back again, Simon?"

"It's not gone, Ella. Look. It's right up there."

It was there all right, but not in the same way. I knew then that the answer was *no*. I'd never get it back. Some things, like innocence, only go one way.

"I want to stop and call Uncle Manny," he said at the corner.

"Don't we still have some of the money Dad gave us?"

Simon shook his head. "The insurance company only pays eighty percent." He indicated my wrists with a glance.

"I'm sorry, Simon."

He stepped inside the phone booth. He held the door open for me, because usually I liked to come in with him, but I only shook my head. It was too crowded in there, with DeeDee, but I couldn't say that. He'd say DeeDee was dead. He'd been saying that a lot lately, and I didn't intend to invite him to say it again.

I heard his words filter through the door, little bits and pieces of them. I tried to shut them out, squinting at the moon, trying to see it the way I had before.

"Well, how is she. . . ? Not at the house, that's for sure. I don't know if this is a good time at all, as far as Ella's concerned. . . . I'll ask her, but if it's too much for her. . . . Yeah, if you would. . . .

I don't know, whatever he can spare. It's been a bad time for money. Yeah, okay. Bye."

He stepped out, and I turned to look at his face, and I saw it just the way I saw the moon, violated, like the loss of innocence, the sort of change that doesn't change back.

"Uncle Manny says Mom's home."

"Oh."

"He says she's a lot better."

"That's good."

"She wants to see us."

"I'm not going back to that house."

"I know. How about if we just had dinner in a restaurant?"

"I guess."

As long as she doesn't touch me, I thought, but I didn't tell Simon that part, figuring it went without saying.

"How do you feel about it, Ella?"

I shrugged, and the subject went away for a minute.

How do you feel things, Simon?

We met at Norm's Restaurant, the same one, on Vermont and Sunset. It was my idea. I thought I'd be comfortable there. Simon put me on the inside booth seat, by the window, and when he sat down, he blocked off my exit.

She looked good, but she didn't feel the same as she looked, the part I could feel across the table. Her hair was nicely combed and curly, and she wore makeup, put on correctly, and red lips, with white teeth showing behind when she smiled.

I never said a word to her, but she kept smiling at me, asking Simon how we both were, and that's when I realized it was coming across the table at me. It was the deepest sense of panic I could imagine, like in that movie *The Blob*, when it's oozing at you, and you know it'll take you over, smother you, eat you alive, but you can't run away.

"Simon, let me out," I hissed in his ear.

"What? Just a second—what'd you say, Mom?"

"Simon, let me out!" Every head in the restaurant turned to look, even the line cooks.

"She probably has to go to the bathroom, Simon. Let her out."

He jumped up and I squeezed past him and ran around the corner toward the restrooms, and kept going. It seemed my only remaining birthright. After all, the nice thing about being a horse is the minimum of options. No fight-or-flight choice involved. Just stretch those muscles, open up the heart and lungs, and don't stop until it's over. My heart was a horse heart. I'd never doubted that.

I stopped at a phone a mile or so down Sunset and called Willie, and asked if she could come pick me up, right away. I couldn't see, I could barely hear her voice on the phone, barely hear my own, and she had to come fast. If Simon and my mother came after me, I'd be a sitting duck. My mother might touch me before I ever saw her coming.

Willie drove over to get me, and took me back to her house, where I asked if I could have a cup of hot chocolate.

"Why did they take the moon away?" I said, maybe a few times, wondering why she didn't answer, until I realized I couldn't hear myself say it.

She brought me a warm mug, but I had to feel for it, and I warmed my hands on it, blowing into it to send steam into my face. I took a big burning gulp but it didn't help. The world stayed black and silent. I felt Willie's hand on my shoulder. No other input from the world outside my head. What a place to be stuck.

"I just realized," I said, or I think I said, "that I came out of her body. And now I think I can save myself by keeping away from her. Don't you see how much too late it is?"

I couldn't tell how loud I was talking, or even if I made a sound at all, but my throat came up strained.

I asked Willie to take me outside into the grass, and she walked with me until I felt it under my shoes, and I fell into it, squeezing tufts between my fingers, knowing it was green from memory.

I rolled around on my back, kicked my legs up in the air, trying to get the feel of it, trying to pretend my neck wasn't too short, and two of my legs weren't arms. I swung back to my feet but it was no use. It didn't balance. It was put together all wrong. I could never be what I was meant to be, because the body was all wrong. Useless.

Useless!

I slammed up against the unyielding stucco of Willie's house, as if I could shatter the worthless shell part of me. As if its obvious defects would run through it like a flaw, causing it to break apart on impact. But for something put together all wrong, it stood surprisingly strong. Willie grabbed me and held me and I knew then, in a sickening flash in my human gut, that I couldn't please them and keep them at the same time, and so would have to disappoint them both.

THE FACE OF SO MUCH CHANGE

EVERETT'S WIFE IS a coal-haired woman named May. She smiles a lot, talks hardly at all.

She serves cornmeal cakes and beans, and canned peaches.

After dinner Everett and I sit out in the dirt in front of his new house, Everett smoking and taking notice of constellations.

I thank him for his hospitality. I want to explain the void it fills in me, how the smallest scrap of hospitality grows to cover vast needs, but it's so much more than Everett would say. Some things, he teaches me with his silence, we must trust others to know.

"How can you walk to the mesa? It's almost fifty miles."

"I've already walked twice that far."

"And your feet and your spirit are still bruised from that. You should wait until you're stronger."

"I can't, Everett. I have to move on. I have to find Sam Roanhorse."

"Then you should let me drive you."

"Well, that just defeats the whole purpose then, Everett. I mean, drive me where? I don't know where my brother Simon is. It's when I get out there. When I just happen to cross a place he's been. It's something I figure out as I go. I can't explain it, but it got me this far, right?"

"Then all the more reason to wait. You need all your resources, not just your feet. You need to travel strong."

"I have to go."

I feel his disappointment, though he says nothing. I have turned away from spirit. Spirit says I should wait. Everything that knows and is right says I must wait. But I have put my brother

Simon above this in my prioritizing, and, even as I am satisfied with that decision, I cannot answer the question of how it is right to place anything before the universe, or how it will benefit me. Or how it will benefit Simon, if there is a Simon.

We sit quiet, and I mark the moment I must rise to go, but my legs seem to take exception to my thinking.

In time we hear the hum of an engine and the crunch of wheels on Everett's rocky dirt road.

An old man with a face like a dried-apple doll jumps down from a one-ton flatbed truck. He walks to where we sit.

Everett says to me, "Your big job has just become easier."

"Everett, I heard the news. Jake says you took your five best pigeons to be bred to the champions in Fort Defiance. Why don't you ever tell me these things yourself? I'm never sure if you're on my side or not."

"Because your birds are faster than mine already." Everett offers the old man a hand-rolled cigarette. "Sam Roanhorse, Ella Ginsberg. Ella Ginsberg, Sam Roanhorse. Ella is wanting to speak with you."

Sam holds the picture for a cautious length of time, away from himself, into the light cast from Everett's new home.

"I can't say this is the man I saw. But I can't say for sure it's not. His hair was yellow, like this, but longer. More tangled. And this man is soft and padded. The man I saw was gaunt, and had not only a mustache but a full beard, untrimmed. Still, if he had traveled far, these changes could happen. But how can I recognize for sure how a man might look in the face of so much change?"

"Mr. Roanhorse, you say he walked north, toward the mesa?"

"Yes, I watched him go. I wondered, does he feel the pain from those blisters of sunburn? What must his feet feel like? Due north to the mesa, without stopping, until he was out of sight."

"Did he say why he wanted the rifle?"

Sam trades a look with Everett, and I know I have asked an unenlightened thing.

"A man who sells rifles asks only if a buyer carries cash. Too many questions are bad for business."

"And he bought ammunition?"

"Yes, a lot of it. A lot to carry. And a big knife. So, what are you going to do now? Will you go look for your brother at the mesa? It's a long walk. In tourist season, when white people drive the roads to Monument Valley and to Canyon de Chelly, you could hitch a ride. Until then, it's quiet. Maybe a Navajo will stop for you, but who knows? You could ride with me back to my store. It's almost twenty miles of the distance."

I glance at Everett, who catches my glance neatly, and I shake my head.

"I appreciate the offer, Mr. Roanhorse, but my host has asked me to stay until I'm stronger. The battle will be better run a few days down the road. And on foot."

"I understand completely," he says, "and good luck to you." He strikes up a long conversation with Everett in Navajo, the upshot of which is that Everett gives him one of the bred pigeons to take back with him. He does not seriously begrudge Sam a piece of his good fortune. At least, this is what I hope I gather.

Everett invites me to sleep in his house, but I say I am happy in my sleeping bag under the stars. I have seen my mistake, and I will pay better attention to the moon and the stars from now on.

He wishes me a good sleep.

THEN:

I KNEW BY the feel of things that I wasn't home. The physical feel, but there was more. The energy of the people around me. Strangers.

Here and there Simon. I knew him across the room, who knows how. Smell, maybe. If Grandma Ginsberg had been there she would have said the extra sense provided by the caul. Thank god she wasn't, though.

Sometimes Willie. I could smell her perfume. She'd sit on the edge of my bed with me, my head dropped back against her, her arm around my shoulder, brushing hair off my face. She'd bring me an apple or a carrot, which I'd eat only while she sat with me. I suppose she'd been told I refused all other food.

Then, after a few days, something terrible happened. It all began to come back. Slowly at first, shadows, whispers. But it grew with time.

It was a bit of a catch-22, I suppose, that the relief of being completely shut down would bring such ease as to open up the door again. Unready to go back, unsure how to cope, I left my eyes unfocused, showed no response to sounds. I heard few sounds, as the other bed in my room remained empty, and no one bothered to talk in my presence, the only exception being Willie.

She would run a monologue the whole time we sat together, metered words with spaces between, which she did not expect me to fill.

"Really not my idea of a good plan, all this, but sometimes, what can you do? The better you get, though, the faster we can get you home. Any sign that you could hear me. It would all help. Any kind of cooperation. Even if you stayed pretty shaky, if you could see and hear, you'd be an outpatient again. Tomorrow. Simon sure wants you home."

I wondered how much she talked to Simon, and what they shared. I wondered if she was testing to see if I could hear her, or just talking to herself. In retrospect I think she tried to support me in some subliminal way, like a person who reads spiritual literature to a coma victim.

I felt sorely tempted, sometimes, to answer her, but I liked her too much. Same with Simon. When someone means too much to me, I want to please them. If I can't, it's hard to be around them at all.

Simon came in one day carrying a cardboard sign, with words on it that he'd made from twigs and glued down. He gave me a hug, then set it on my lap and placed my hands on the letters.

I could see the words, though a bit narrow and shaded, and I could see Simon, but I wasn't sure if I was ready to give it all up yet. So I ran my hand over each letter, one slow step at a time, but I knew what it said.

It said, *We'll stay together, even when you're well.*

"What about your wife, Simon?"

He jumped at the sound, maybe because it was unexpected, or maybe it was too loud. Everything still sounded like my ears were plugged and ringing, and I couldn't tell if I used too much volume.

"Can you hear me, Ella?"

"A little bit."

"Have you been able to hear all along?"

"No, just the last couple of days."

"Lots of married couples have parents who live with them, and most of them have children, so why not a sister?"

"Are you going to have children, Simon?"

129

"No. Hell no. Not me. Are you kidding? You wouldn't have kids, would you, Ella?"

"I'm not even going to have a husband."

"Now, don't say that. You don't know."

"No kids."

"It's a pact, then," he said. "No kids."

"DeeDee was a pact, too."

"Oh, now, Ella, don't start. It seemed okay at the time, but I think it's part of what's keeping you sick. Not every—" But the door snapped shut again. I couldn't see or hear him, or tell when he'd given up and gone.

On the day I was released, Willie told me I'd been in the hospital for sixteen days. I was surprised. I'd lost all landmarks of time, and those sixteen days seemed to fill a whole era, like the time it would take to live out a failed relationship or attend high school.

That was the day the shaking started. I never told anyone about it. Not even Willie. It was a deep sort of a tremble, all the way down in my gut. It wasn't a scared kind of shaking, or the shiver you get from cold. It was fatigue. Strain. Like the time I helped my father strip all the linoleum off the kitchen floor, and then when I sat down to dinner my hands were so tired I couldn't hold my fork still.

At first I shook almost all the time, except in Willie's room at County Mental Health, where we met five days a week, and in bed at night.

Later I only felt it when I had to be around real people, and it was important not to be myself, or when Simon saw me acting strange and I had to try to do better.

A month or so after I left the hospital, Willie and I made a pact. I had more confidence in her, because she hadn't broken one yet.

The deal was that she would never give me a hard time about DeeDee, or harp at me that she's gone, or ask me to give her up, if I would simply accept what was real about her and what wasn't. I could talk to her and listen to her, but every time I did, I had to understand that she was not really there, even if she seemed to be.

At first I had to admit that I didn't know what was real about DeeDee and what wasn't, but Willie said no problem, I could just act as if I did, and maybe it would get to be a habit.

"Just practice," she said.

After that, every time DeeDee said something to me, or every time I moved over to leave room for her, I'd say, in the privacy of my head: *You're not real.*

It went fine for a while, then I realized she wasn't arguing with me.

And my sister DeeDee, if she was real and I said she wasn't, would have me for breakfast. I'd be just so much dead meat at that point. But day after day I called her *unreal* and survived. My life got heavier then, and I spent more time in bed. Even dressing and brushing my teeth caused me to tremble from exertion, because I knew it meant I had to go outside, which meant I had to go see Willie, because that's the only time I ever went out. I didn't mind going to see Willie, but I minded going out onto the street, and I minded riding the bus. It made my heart pound and my insides feel like a building about to collapse in an earthquake.

My initial solution came in the form of night rovings, like an owl or a coyote. I had been stagnating in the house too long, and some glowing ball of spirit in me threatened to fade to nothing, and I feared it might be like fire—you need fire to make fire, and you must never let the last of it die.

I found Griffith Park, at three A.M., a safe environment. It was closed, of course, which meant I almost never ran into anyone, except an occasional pair of lovers, but only occasional. Most

131

lovers preferred ground they didn't have to reach on foot. Only the animals seemed to move and breathe with me, and although the city lived in lights beneath the hills where I perched, it always looked manageable from the distance.

Most important was my communion with the moon. As damaged merchandise we had a lot in common. But the moon taught me something, one of those pivotal somethings you tell your poor bored grandchildren when you've told them already, except that I'd never have any.

The moon taught me that only madness is pure. Once I'd made a start without it, my life was trodden territory, never really mine. At first I found this depressing, a sense of loss I could barely feel but which sapped me. In time I grew used to the feeling, which made it possible to bring more feet into my impure mind to track things up. If I couldn't go back, I might as well go forward.

I tried to pay attention in my sessions with Willie, to see if this revelation brought change. I might have even thrown out a few experimental wanderings, just to see if I was feeling any braver.

"I've been noticing something about my brother Simon. I've been staring at him a lot. I think it makes him nervous, but he won't say so."

I stared at Willie, but it didn't bother her. She wore a pink blouse that day, with a gray jacket over it, and where the pink showed through it looked smooth, like satin. I noticed she seemed relaxed around me, as if talking to an adult. Her eyes eased all the way into calm.

"What do you notice about him?"

That was the moment I would have to find words for it, which seemed tricky.

"You know how if you ask a kid to write a story, the people they create are always missing something? They only do and say exactly what's necessary for the story. They never scratch their ears with a pencil eraser, or whistle stupid songs, or snap their gum. They never have beer bottle collections or facial tics."

"They're not three-dimensional. Is that what you mean?"

I sat back and sighed, glancing over her gray shoulder to the horses. *Help me out, guys. My brain is handicapped with too many thoughts. I'm too human to say what I mean.*

"I'm not sure who Simon is. I keep watching him, waiting for him to do something that's pure Simon, and nobody else."

"What do you make of that, Ella?"

"I don't know what to make of it. That's why I brought it up. But I worry about him. Mrs. Hurley used to worry about Simon. Did I ever tell you that?"

Willie raised her eyebrows just the tiniest bit. If I wasn't staring and assessing, I might never have noticed. I realized later that she could have said, *no, you never told me anything about Mrs. Hurley. Not one word. You didn't even know who she was or what became of her.* But Willie was smart.

She said, "I don't think so."

"The last thing she said to me before she died is that she always worries about the ones who say everything is okay. Don't you think that's kind of an interesting thing to say?"

A little tremor started in my belly, and I set off in another direction, and she let me go.

She didn't repeat what I'd said, or rub my nose in it.

After a few minutes of discussion about my brother Simon, we agreed that I had enough to worry about with me.

Willie and Simon put their heads together in the fall, and enrolled me in night school. All the other students were grown men and women. Most seemed humbled by the experiences of a high school freshman, and nobody gave me a hard time. In fact, I became something of a mascot with fellow students and teachers, the thirteen-year-old kid who acted and talked forty.

If they knew that my emotional problems had sent me into their midst, it was never mentioned.

HAWKS AND RABBITS

IN THE MORNING the air is cool, the ground hard. The sun peers over the horizon with no spoken threats.

Then, as if looking into a mirror, the old mare comes to bump my face with her muzzle. She's a battered white paint, short bristly mane, prominent ribs, chocolate patches on her neck and withers. She knows she is at home here, and questions me only slightly.

I wish her a good morning and run my fingers up her face, into her forelock.

Everett Ankeah comes out to wish me the same, bringing hot soup and half a wheel of fry bread.

"So, I see you and Yozzy are acquainted, and I needn't make introductions."

I thank him for the breakfast, and sit up to take the hot soup. I look around me and ask what keeps Yozzy close to home. "I don't see any fences."

"That's because there are no fences. I don't fence my wife in, but she stays with me. And if she didn't, what could I do? All down this road you'll see signs: *Watch for animals.* The sheep and horses range free. They know their homes."

He sits with me while I finish my breakfast, though there seems nothing more to say. I'm glad for his company, but I trust him to know that.

"Is there anything I can do for you, Everett, that would mean as much as this food means to me?"

"Well, there's a lot of work to be done in the diner."

I nod my assent without further comment. I'm learning.

I help Everett throw an old car seat on the back of his truck, with some other trash to take to the dump, and he pulls a knife from his belt, slashes through the naugahyde, and cuts two thick pieces of foam rubber, which we duct-tape to the knees of my jeans.

"I'll take the high road," he says, and we work together on the kitchen area, even as I stay off my healing feet.

I clean grease off the back of the deep-fat fryer, years of grime from the inside bottom of the refrigerator cases.

"I see what you mean about the old owner," I say, and he grunts his disgust.

We work like this day after day, breaking when May brings food and drink, and at noon for a two-hour nap. We talk little, as little needs to be said.

On the fourth day, Everett Ankeah says this:

"I had a strange dream last night. I saw your brother Simon's camp—a makeshift tent near the mesa. The tent looked like it was made from skin. Like mule deer skin. He had a fire burning in front."

I wait to see if he'll continue, but he doesn't.

"Thank you for telling me that, Everett, but it could be symbolic, too. Don't you agree? Dreams so often are. The skin might be a symbol for the passageway between this world and the next."

It surprises me to hear myself say this, but I do it because I don't dare believe. It's an old habit, to refuse to hope for the best.

"Yes, that's possible. Maybe I'm only wasting your time in telling you."

I say nothing. We clean in silence for another hour.

"One more thing," he says, "that I learned from this dream. Your guide is not the hawk. Your guide is the rabbit."

I laugh when he says this, not at him, or the idea, but at myself, because I should have known.

"The hawk threw me off," I say. "By being too helpful."

"Maybe you needed something closer to your own ideas." I'm not sure what he means by that, but I don't have to ask because he sees the question in my face. "Just as no one likes to think he was a common laborer in a past life, no one wants to take the advice of a lowly rabbit."

"I'm all ears," I say, and he laughs, as though I meant it as a pun, which I didn't.

That night, as I tuck into my sleeping bag, Everett squats smoking by the porch and Yozzy sleeps on her feet close by, ears laid back along her narrow neck.

I face north, and stare through black night at Simon's mesa. My feet are only the slightest bit better than when I arrived at Everett's, barely able to take my weight. My goal feels suddenly impossible. Fifty miles might just as well be a thousand.

Above the mesa, I see the knowing face of the man in the moon, and he makes me cry, because he tells the truth this time, of what he knows. The trip is beyond me.

Everett must hear me cry, because he comes to squat beside me.

"You need to leave now," he says.

"I can't walk that far."

"I know. I can't let you take my truck—I need it."

"I never meant that you should. And you know I couldn't find what I'm looking for in a truck." If I thought I could, I would have kept my own.

"But I will let you take my horse. She'll stay with you. She respects you. She's very old, but if you can find enough water, she'll take you there. If you survive, and she survives, bring her back to me. If not I'll say a prayer for you both."

When I wake in the morning, Yozzy wears a leather hackamore with rope reins, and a woven blanket.

She nudges me insistently, as if anxious to leave.

THEN:

I GRADUATED FROM high school after three years, an example of the reapplication of self. I learned some interesting things there. For example, I learned that restless middle-aged married men will always be drawn to me, almost against their will, like ants drawn to a scoop of ice cream when it's wasted on the pavement. Grandma Ginsberg's true flesh and blood, I pulled those strings, received their attention, and gave nothing back, unless my acknowledgment of their attention was all they really needed.

It seemed an odd lesson in visibility, a subject I knew little about. The more boring the class, the more likely I might turn to catch a man staring at me. I courted attention like fire, fascinated and afraid. I hated it, lured it, played with it, tossed it back. It created a hypervigilance slow to wear away. I was most comfortable when least seen.

During my three years of night school, I worked days for Lois and Herbie Greenblatt, owners of Greenblatt's Delicatessen in Hollywood. My job was easy and normally stress-free. Trot to work in jeans, a white T-shirt and a white cap, both displaying ads for my employer. Pick up a paper bag, with a bill stapled on. Or two bags, or three. Stuff them with napkins, extra for the office on Hollywood and Bronson. Run these bags to their destinations, return to find more.

The Greenblatts liked me, and paid a dollar thirty-five an hour, which I doubled with tips. The customers were friendly because they were hungry, and I learned to run fast.

On the rare occasions someone gave me a hard time, I became invisible, or sicced Lois Greenblatt on them, or both.

The time that stands out, a man named Larry in a camera store on Hollywood Boulevard decided I had brought him the wrong sandwich. Four people from his store had ordered all at once; everybody's order came up fine except his. He said he ordered ham, not corned beef. I shouldn't have laughed out loud, but if he'd called Greenblatt's and ordered ham, Lois would have called him a few choice names in Yiddish and hung up the phone. Anybody knows that.

He yelled at me. "Well, you just screwed it up."

His dark eyebrows tried to knit together in the center. He had a strange nose that seemed to grow upon itself, like a cancer. I didn't even make up the orders—Herbie did—but I couldn't say that. I just made myself disappear.

As soon as I did, he turned on his heels, as though disgusted to have no one left to yell at. That's how I knew it worked.

I ran back to the store without the money for the rest of the order. I thought Lois would be mad at me, but I couldn't bring myself to disappear on her. I owed Lois better than that.

I told her the story. She got on the phone and asked for "this Larry," and while she waited, her big round face reddened, and she smoothed her huge apron, as if to keep life in order.

"Now, listen, you, we don't have ham sandwiches at Greenblatt's. We're a kosher deli, got that? *Kosher.* Next time you want to order from us you got to pay what you all should have paid today, except you chased my girl away. She's a kid, see? You see this? You think she's the owner? The manager? No, she *schleps* orders. You yell at her one more time you get your lunch someplace else."

She slammed down the phone and the ringer resonated among the silent clientele. A force to reckon with, that Lois.

"You go right back out," she said, stuffing a bag into my hand, "don't lose your nerve." On the way out the door I overheard her tell Herbie, "I just thought who she reminds me of. Benny, that's who." I had never heard of Benny.

Nobody thought the camera store would order again, but they did. They paid me for the previous time, along with a two-dollar tip, and Larry had to sit in the corner until I was gone, like a bad dog. I watched the angle of his face, and when it swept around toward me I went away in my head, and sure enough, he looked right through me like I was a window onto something better.

That was a great turning point for me. I ran those streets like I owned them, head tucked down to watch the streak of sidewalk cracks rush by. I watched them accumulate like shares of stock, reminding me I had as much right to this city as anyone.

Because if anyone challenged my ownership, I could be gone.

When I got back from my last run, Herbie was sitting in his office, an unmarked corner of the storeroom, doing his books.

"Pull up a chair," he said. He liked to talk to me at the end of the day, get a sense of how everything had gone.

There were no chairs, but I pulled up a carton of halvah and sat with my knees tucked up against my chin, my breath still coming in puffs.

"You're in good shape," he said. He twisted a corner of his mustache. Folds and billows of Herbie pushed out against his clothes. He wore normal-sized pants that rode far below his great belly. His eyes laughed, even when I saw nothing to laugh about. Like Santa Claus, though god knows I would never say this to Herbie.

"So, how did your day go, young lady?"

"Fine, Herbie. Good. I made seven dollars in tips."

"See, the customers like you, Ella. That's good for everybody."

I saw, over Herbie's desk, a photo of a dog tacked on the bulletin board. I'd seen it before. Beside it hung photos of their two grown children, forty-year-olds with friendly, unintimidating faces, but I liked the dog best. A silly-looking dog, really. Sort of a wire-haired terrier, only no sort in particular. All the different breeds seemed to argue in this one poor little mutt, sending his hair in a wealth of directions. His head hung down, as if cowed by the camera, and the flash lit up his eyes devil red, which didn't look at home on him at all.

This time Herbie saw me looking.

"That's Benny, god rest his soul."

"That's Benny?"

"The one and only."

I asked Herbie to tell me all about Benny.

"So, what about him? Good friend. Cried like babies when he passed on, both of us. Why? What do you want to know?"

"How was Benny like me?"

Herbie's chair groaned under his weight as he shifted back into it. His eyes didn't see the joke anymore.

"You weren't supposed to hear that, you know, but it wasn't an insult. You could do worse than to be like Benny. It's just . . . we got him out of the pound, and he always had this look in his eyes. Always braced for the worst even when everything was dandy. We never knew what had happened to him, but it must've been really bad, you know? That's all Lois meant by that. No disrespect."

"It's okay, Herbie, I don't mind."

I found it flattering, that I reminded someone of their dog.

"Take a sandwich before you go. Take two, one for your brother. Here, I'll make it myself. What'll you have, roast beef? Corned beef? Pastrami?"

"Roast beef is Simon's favorite."

I watched through the glass case as Herbie assembled the sandwiches, thicker with meat than any he sold.

"Tell your brother Simon we send our regards."

Simon wasn't home yet. I took a bath and got dressed for school, and ate my sandwich without him. I wondered if he'd gotten Friday off from work, for his birthday, and if I should have asked Herbie for Friday off just in case.

Sometime around six-thirty I began to suspect it would be one of those nights I'd miss Simon entirely. It happened once or twice a week. I left his sandwich on our only table, with a note that said Herbie and Lois sent their regards.

Then I heard the knock.

I held still, nothing more at first. Nobody ever knocked on our door. Ever. Not even the landlord, because Simon always paid for our room on the first of the month, never made him come to us. I slid over to the door and hooked the safety chain.

"Who's there?"

"Is that you, Ella?"

"Dad?"

"Yeah, let me in, sweetie."

"Dad?"

"Yeah, it's me, Ella. Open the door."

"Dad, how did you find us?"

"Honey, I always knew where you were. You think it's hard to find where somebody is? You think I'd let my own kids go off where I couldn't even keep an eye on them? Why aren't you opening the door, Ella?"

"Simon's not here."

"So? I got a present. For his birthday. I want him to come to the house Friday, but even if he won't, he can still have the present. Just open up, sweetie."

"Simon doesn't let me open the door while he's away."

Actually, it had never come up before, but it sounded damned convincing.

"But it's your father."

I leaned on the door, my shoulder wedged against it, as though latch, deadbolt and chain would not do the job unaided, but then I felt it come right through the door at me. Like *The Blob*, only worse, because *The Blob* is only a movie.

I jumped back away from the door. The room had only one exit, the one my father contaminated. I unlocked the door. I allowed it to drift open slightly, and as he pushed it, I darted under his arm and ran. I drew myself in, tried to disappear, but it didn't work. Not on him. He tried to follow me, but I lost him by cutting around the side of the house.

A spot on my shoulder burned as if I'd touched his jacket, or even his aura, on my dangerous trip through his diseased space. I ran all the way to Sunset Boulevard, caught the bus in the direction opposite of school, got off at Silver Lake Boulevard and walked the mile to Willie's. She answered the door in her robe and socks. She'd been eating dinner.

"I should call first, shouldn't I?"

"Yes, in the future I'd appreciate that. This time it just so happens your timing is okay."

She doesn't want you here, DeeDee said, but I went in anyway. DeeDee said lots of things I'd learned to ignore.

Willie ate the last little bits of her TV dinner, then threw away the foil tray.

"What's up, Ella?"

I couldn't say. I wanted her to tell me how to cleanse the spot on my shoulder without breaking my promise. I wanted to use her shower, to wash myself twenty or thirty times, as people who feel violated tend to do. But I knew it wouldn't help. Because it was so much too late. I was his own flesh and blood; what made me think I could duck at this late date?

I said I wanted to stay until Simon got home.

She drove me back and walked up with me. Simon was home, resting his head on the table, clutching a set of car keys on a ring in his right hand. Keys I'd never seen before, not his regular ones.

He picked up his head, nodded to Willie.

"I can't believe he knew where we were this whole time."

"He could be lying, Simon. I mean, if he knew all along, why did he miss all those other birthdays?"

"He said twenty-one was too big to let go by. He gave me his Oldsmobile. Only four years old."

"I bet he didn't know all along."

"He knows now."

Years later, after we'd moved, Simon confided that our father had threatened him, said he could take me back if Simon didn't keep in closer touch.

At the time, with me only fifteen and still feeling a little on the edge, he never mentioned that part at all.

UNTIL AND UNLESS

I WATCH EVERETT Ankeah's hands, his fingers as they lace together, his rough palms lined with calluses, like grain on fine wood. I see the rings of calluses as tree rings, revealing Everett's true age. I press my left knee into those palms, and he slings me up to Yozzy's back. I ease gently down onto her. After all, it is her back. Not a motorcycle seat, or a bale of straw, but the fine vertebrae of a sentient being.

Everett hands up my bedroll, which crinkles with something that did not use to belong to me. He has made additions to my bedroll. I hang it by its rope, over my shoulder.

Something pulls at me, hurting me, as I stare down into Everett's ageless face. It makes me postpone the moment of moving on.

"Do you and May have children, Everett?"

It seems a foolish time to ask, but the alternative is to nudge Yozzy's sides and head north. I feel the warmth of the Ankeah home at my back.

"Four."

"Where?"

"Grown and gone."

"You don't look old enough to have four children grown and gone." In part this is true, all but the ageless part.

"I told my children the same thing, but they defied me and grew to adulthood."

"Kids," I say, and Everett smiles.

I reach my hand down to him and he grasps it, and we hold on. I want to say thank you, but his eyes remind about redundancy.

"We'll pray for rain," he says.

"He-rain," I say. I know all about Navajo He-rain. Well, not all about it. I know what Everett told me about it, and all I need to know. I know that without it we might die.

Yozzy turns her head and bumps my leg with her muzzle. She's right, of course. I allow her to move off toward Simon's mesa.

My legs hang loosely against the blanket and her bony sides. I do not tell her which way to go. She tells me. She has seen me stare. She feels the pull as surely as I do.

She moves with Navajo grace down the hard dirt shoulder of the highway, and I look back. Yozzy does not.

I look back because I felt at home with May and Everett, as much as I ever have anywhere. I don't want that time to be gone. But it is gone, and even if I had not left, still it would be gone. Only for the time I was meant to be there could I feel so at peace.

As the sun rises to taunt me, to sweat the truth from me, I think about Willie, asking me if I loved anyone. Did I love the Greenblatts? Mrs. Hurley? Simon?

I said I figured I must, but I don't think that answer rings the bell. What would it feel like, I said, if I did?

Then later, after I'd met Shane, I ran into Willie's little room at Mental Health, and said I had it now. Someone I knew I loved.

"How do you know?"

"Well, because . . . I do."

"But you still haven't figured out if you love Simon, and you're closer to him than anybody."

"No, I do love Simon."

"But you can't feel it."

"But I feel it with Shane."

By the end of the session, she had introduced the possibility of lust, offered to muddy the water, to further confuse the issue.

Maybe real love is the one you can't feel.

I look back again, to see Everett's house fade to a pinpoint on the horizon. I wonder if I love Everett and May, and if someday

I'll answer that question without having the example ripped away first.

Yozzy bumps my knee with her muzzle, a clear way to say, *stop that.* Yozzy has loved Everett longer than I have, but she puts one steady hoof in front of another and doesn't look back. But then, Yozzy is a horse, for which I envy her.

We see no cars, no trucks, no travelers. We see only a flock of dingy white sheep, herded and protected by two lone dogs. They flow like a river across the highway, leaping and colliding in a fluid, choreographed procession.

The rear dog barks at the rudeness, the intrusion of our presence. He stands in the center of the highway, chastising us, daring us, vocal in his indignation. His rough coat is mottled in three colors, the white of his bib is surprisingly white.

Yozzy cuts a silent deal with him, winding just as far around his flock as he asks her to. I realize I am still a stranger in this place, and I thank Yozzy with a pat on the neck, for knowing so much that I don't. For teaching me.

A brown jackrabbit skitters across the road, then turns north, to Simon's mesa, bowing away from the highway, and Yozzy bows with him, and continues walking. I would not presume to steer.

I scan the sky for signs of rain, but the sky is a pale blue, no cloud in sight, and the sun laughs at me. I want to go home, but until and unless I find Simon, I don't know where that might be.

THEN:

EVEN WITH MY eyes closed, I knew Shane was there, just off my left elbow. I felt him there. When I opened my eyes I saw the sun sink below the stubby wall that separated the pool from the parking lot, and beyond that, the high, forbidding wall of Paramount Studios, just across Gower from Simon's and my new home. Shane and I sat poolside, alone. The other guys were all at work, except for sleeping Jason, and Eddie and Paul, upstairs in Eddie's apartment, cooking a donated pork roast for that night's communal apartment house dinner.

Simon came through with Sarah, from the parking lot to the sliding glass door that separated our living room from the pool. Simon worked a part-time job in the evenings. I worked two jobs, so Simon could go to school and become an astronomer.

I was seventeen years old, a high school graduate. I sent Simon back to school after a dream I had, the night after my own graduation. In this dream I sat with Mrs. Hurley on the porch swing, at her old house in Columbus. Mrs. Hurley pulled nips from a bottle of apricot brandy, and we rocked that old porch swing until it creaked. I thought she'd come to deliver advice, but she said nothing at all. Later, upon waking, I knew she'd delivered all the advice I'd ever need, years before, and had come only to offer a timely reminder.

Moving to the new place had been my idea. The new place had a bedroom. Simon wouldn't take it, choosing to entertain Sarah in the living room, at the odd times his schedule might permit.

"We won't need a bedroom until we're married," he had said.

It was at City College that Simon had met Sarah, though I didn't realize he had at first, either because he never brought her home to our little room, as I suspect, or because I was gone to work when he did, or both. He had cut classes one Friday afternoon, because the Greenblatts closed early on Friday for the Sabbath, and had taken us both out to lunch as an introduction.

I couldn't see anything about her that required an introduction. She looked like Simon, only female, and the energy she sent across the table, though probably not on purpose, felt like Simon, which felt like me. She had always existed there between us, as though our energy had expanded outward until Sarah appeared. She bent over backwards to be nice to me, and I wanted to tell her I'd like her anyway, just to save her the trouble, but there's no point arguing with somebody who's trying to be nice to you.

I got a club sandwich and a cherry Coke out of the deal, and when she left to go back to class, I told him he'd spend the rest of his life with Sarah, and he said, "I know." I knew he knew, I just wanted him to know that I knew. Then he assured me that we'd still always be together.

I left for my appointment with Willie, and sat on the windowsill in her plain room, and talked about Simon, and Sarah, and our future, and rolled the denim of my jeans into little scrolls, until I noticed she was watching. I'd never been troubled by nervous habits, ever, so I stopped, not wanting Willie to think this meant anything in particular.

I stared out the window, onto the ivy hill, the edge of the freeway pavement, trying to talk, the way I always did, saying nothing at all.

Then I said, "We won't always be together, you know."

"You're worried that Sarah will pull you apart."

I said, "No," and I meant it. Sarah wouldn't do anything to us. Life would pull us apart. Because we were not the same person, my brother Simon and I, and we would not appear in all the same places at all the same times. I didn't worry this—I knew it.

Now, by the pool, Simon greeted us. "Hi, Ella," he said. "Hi, Shane," and he smiled at me, and Sarah smiled, and then they were inside our apartment, gone. I had seen my brother Simon, a notable occasion.

Simon didn't mind when I sat with Shane or Jason, or most other men in the building, but a few of my new friends made him uncomfortable. Shane and Jason had been married over a year, but Eddie and Paul were promiscuous, according to Simon. He had to approve of Shane and Jason—otherwise, how could he show he wasn't homophobic? I had once accused him of this, using one of many words I learned from my new friends.

Maybe Simon didn't like Eddie and Paul because he couldn't understand them when they talked about butches and queens, and men they referred to as "Grand Canyons," and the cans of Crisco which appeared in every apartment, usually not in the kitchen. Or maybe because they talked rough sometimes, maybe because he overheard the conversation about Mario Black, which transpired in my presence.

"What the fuck do I care how good he looks?" Eddie had said. "You know what he does? I mean, what he doesn't do? He doesn't fuck, he doesn't suck. You suck him—that's it."

And Paul said, "Well, fuck him."

To which Shane replied, "No, he doesn't do that," then nudged Paul in the ribs and motioned in my direction. Shane reminded them sometimes how to talk in front of me. I liked it, though. I liked the way they talked, like it was okay for me to be there, like I was around, only not enough to hurt. But I also liked the way Shane reminded.

Simon must have picked up the Mario Black conversation, because he stamped into the house, unwilling to catch my eye. Shane said, "There's just no pleasing some people."

He said this in reference to Simon's watchdog approach when he had thought they were all straight.

I had celebrated the end of the moving by buying a new bathing suit, and jumping in the pool, and lounging around to tan like all my new friends. Simon was away at school so much he didn't even see the suit I'd bought, not for three days, and when he did, he hit the ceiling.

He sat on the edge of my chaise lounge, so nobody would hear how mad he was. "You're seventeen years old, you're the only girl in the whole building, and I just don't like the way these guys look at you. Not one bit."

So I looked around to see what he meant, but no one was looking at me. And as I looked around, Simon looked around too, and saw the same. A young red-haired man flashed Simon a big white smile that looked shy and searching, and Simon marched back inside without another word.

It was true, what Shane said, that Simon was getting harder to please. In fact, I had a date that same night to go dancing with Paul and Eddie, but I would have to tell Simon it was Shane and Jason. Shane had to work, I knew that. But Simon didn't know.

"You sure you can't go?" I asked Shane, taking that moment to look at him again. I loved to look at Shane.

"Sorry, Ella, wish I could. Why? You worried about going?" Shane always knew.

Shane was James Dean, only much better, in jeans and heavy black boots, and a white T-shirt, and a black leather jacket, worn and scuffed and faded to gray at the elbows. Not now, at the pool, but nearly always. And dark hair combed back with one loose strand falling into his eyes, and thin, strong arms with little muscles bulging at the top, at moments like this, and the best tan of anybody, which he'd show off by peeling back the leg of his trunks for contrast.

Shane was a whole choir of voices, all hitting the same perfect note, and everybody who hears it feels the spirit, and comes to life in everybody else.

Shane was everything in the world, except those things I already had, and I had so little.

After a while, when I took over my shift from Jason at the Lucky K Market, I would wonder if it was fair to like Jason, and be his friend, and have fantasies about him dying suddenly, all at the same time. I asked Willie, and that's when we got to talking about Shane, and once we got started, it seemed like it might never stop.

"So what're you scared of?" Shane asked next.

"Well, maybe asking Simon."

"Come on," he said. "I'll go with you."

"But you're seventeen," was Simon's immediate answer.

"Gino's is a chicken coop," I said, and treated Simon as naïve for not understanding that reference. "You know, chicken. Underage. They don't serve alcohol there."

Actually, alcohol or no, you had to be eighteen, but Eddie was only seventeen, and Paul was barely eighteen and he'd been going to Gino's for three years.

"I guess," he said, and then Shane and I stood outside in the hall, which smelled of amyl nitrate, because the guys in 102 bottled and sold the stuff. It made the backs of my eyes feel numb, and my brain thick.

"What if he'd said no?"

"I'd still have gone."

Simon worked and went to school so much, I really only asked his permission as a courtesy.

Shane invited me into his apartment—Jason slept behind a closed bedroom door—and asked what I was still scared of. I never asked him how he knew these things.

I told him I didn't know how to dance, and he laughed and put on a Spinners record, and told me nobody knows how to dance, because there's no right or wrong way. He danced for me through two songs. After a while I tried to imitate him, and he said I was already better than half the guys at Gino's.

I tried it in front of his mirror, and got so depressed I had to go sit down on the couch.

"Hey, come on," he said. "You were doing okay."

"But I hate my hair and my face and I look like a jerk, even when I'm not dancing."

Shane stood me up in front of the mirror and pulled one of his big, V-neck white T-shirts over my own. It hung like a dress. Then he gently twisted up my hair in back and slipped a white painter's cap over it, pulling the brim down partway over my eyes. And in the final touch, which made me gasp, he took off his black leather jacket and put it on me.

"What do you think?"

"Wow." It was all I could say. I had no experience, no preparation, for liking myself in front of a mirror. "But I can't wear your leather jacket to Gino's."

"Sure you can. I can't wear it at work, anyway. But be careful with it. Don't set it down anywhere and turn your back."

"I'll never take it off. I promise."

He showed me how to push the sleeves up above my elbows, but then I looked in the mirror and saw my ugly bands of scar tissue, and I told him I liked it better flopping over my hands.

He turned the cuffs back one turn.

"What'd you do to your wrists, Ella?"

Nobody had ever asked me that before. Everybody wanted to ask, I could tell, but nobody ever did.

"Oh. I burned myself."

"By accident?"

He turned me to face him, flipped the collar up around my ears.

"I don't know. Not really. It was a mistake, I guess, but not an accident."

"That's what I thought." He turned me back to the mirror and I looked so damned good, so in control, with his hands on my shoulders and his face right beside mine. "First time I saw you, I thought, here's a girl who's been to hell and back again."

I smiled at Shane's eyes in the mirror. "I don't know if I'm back yet."

He kissed me on the temple. "Just keep putting one foot in front of the other, Ella. It'll happen."

I heard Jason's voice then, breaking my world apart, calling from the bedroom. "Sha-ane," as if it had two syllables, "you're either coming to bed or you're not, honey."

I left with Shane's hat and jacket. It was more than I'd ever expected. It wasn't enough.

OWNERS OF THE DREAM

THE SUN IS merciless overhead. Time to rest in the shade, but there is no shade. There is no water. Why do I think there ever will be?

Reaching deep into the unfamiliar sensation, I see that I am afraid. This is a good sign. If Willie were here, she'd be proud of me. Simon will be proud, too, if there is a Simon.

My fear is that there won't be, but I am just as afraid for myself. I'm afraid to die out here, afraid to survive. I'm afraid of the pain of heat and thirst without relief. More than anything, I'm afraid Yozzy will die. Then I'll be alone. Without her heart to fortify my own, without her judgment, her heroism, her horseness.

She begins to drag her front hooves and stumble, and I slide to the ground. If we can't rest in the shade, we will have to rest in the sun.

I turn Yozzy free to graze on the dry, scrubby grass, and I unroll my sleeping bag. I find a parcel of white butcher's paper, and, inside, a thick stack of beef jerky in uneven sheets.

I mouth silent gratitude for Everett and May and eat one piece. I set my little packet of belongings aside and stretch out, pulling out the photo of Simon. I wonder why I still carry it. Because it strikes me that if Simon exists at all, he does not exist as the man in the photo. He has changed, inside and out. If this was not true, he'd be home with his wife Sarah. And I'd be at work, because I'd be my old self, which I'm not. This is no time for a frozen image of Simon, or of myself. We are fluid, like the sky. Like water, if I ever see water again.

I lie awake for hours before I fall asleep, then I wake suddenly. Even with my eyes open, squinting, watching Yozzy graze, I still see the dream.

I see a cave opening, covered with a flap of animal skin, which moves in the breeze. I know the cave is Simon's house, but Simon is not home. I see a fire burning inside, see it flicker and glow through the skin, but I never see Simon. Only the wind in attendance; the dream fades.

Maybe the dream was sent to me by Everett. *If you're that good, Everett, send rain.*

We walk half a mile before I find a rock big enough to ease me onto Yozzy's back. Muscles inside my thighs scream in chorus with my feet.

We ride until the sun dips away. My mouth is thick and dry, my head fuzzy. I want to find the road, because the road might lead us to Sam Roanhorse's store. Surely we must have traveled close to twenty miles. But the road is gone, I can't even guess in which direction.

I have never completely believed in a god, but suddenly I hope there is one, and that he knows where we are.

As the first pale star appears on the horizon, I pick up my head from a half-nap against Yozzy's neck. I see a house. Yozzy has found a house.

I make out a man on the front porch, smoking a pipe, and he steps down and walks to greet us. I blink my eyes, recognize the dried-apple-doll face, but it is not a dream. It stays.

He reaches out to pat Yozzy's shoulder.

"So, Ella Ginsberg, we meet again."

In Sam Roanhorse's sink, I fill a stewpot with water and carry it out to Yozzy, who drinks her fill.

"Give her another one later," he says. "Not all at once."

When Yozzy is satisfied, I accept a glass and drink.

My leg muscles stiffen, and it hurts to sit at his table.

Sam opens a can of corned beef hash and fries up three thick slices, topping them with a cooked egg from his own chickens. He sets this feast in front of me, and for the first time in my life I feel I'd like to pray silently before taking my meal.

"Are all Navajo this hospitable, Mr. Roanhorse?"

He smiles. He says, "The Navajo are a good people, like everybody else. I don't think there's such a thing as a bad people. This isn't about us, Ella. It's about you. Can't you see?"

I wipe my mouth on my napkin, and Sam pours red wine into my empty cup. He must know by now that I can't see.

"You have a mission. Most of us only wish we did. It's the purest, most untarnished way to live a life. All the universe envies you. All the people, the animals, even the sun and the clouds and the night. If we could trade places with you, we would. So we line up at your back in admiration. We are all with you, Ella."

He offers me his couch for the night. I thank him but decline. Night is the time to travel.

He offers me a bottle to carry water, but I refuse. I choose to believe he knows why. He must see that every pound of water I carry increases Yozzy's burden. I can't carry enough for her— only for myself. I will not make her way heavy to lighten my own. It is enough to borrow her feet.

I place my knee in Sam's laced fingers, swing onto Yozzy's back. She is refreshed now; I feel it. We are ready to continue.

I reach my hand down to grasp that of my host.

He says, "Last night I had a dream. I dreamed I saw your brother Simon."

"Where?"

"Where? I don't know. Somewhere around here. Up near the mesa, maybe. I didn't think much about where. I guess he had a camp somewhere around here."

"And he was in it? I mean, Simon was there?"

"I think he was."

In his dream, no skin. In Everett's and mine, no Simon. I like Sam's dream the best. "That dream gets around," I say.

"A dream has more than one owner. It belongs to everyone it may choose to touch. Whomever it concerns."

I say goodbye to Sam and move off toward the mesa.

I feel the warmth of the Roanhorse home at my back, but I don't turn to look.

THEN:

THREE FRIDAY NIGHTS dancing at Gino's and I became something of a status symbol. The guys tripped all over each other for the privilege of dancing with me, some for the novelty, I figured, or to show a liberal bent, others to thumb their noses at their own dates and lovers.

I got kisses on the cheeks, on the forehead, sometimes on the lips, and no matter how much they fawned over me, I never felt the need to hide away.

On the third Friday, I wore Shane's jacket again, but I left the cap at home. I'd gone to a salon on Sunset Boulevard, and had my hair cut off short, and thinned, and I wore it slicked back, so the waves lay flat along my skull, like a freeze-frame of a wind-blown wheat field, only darker.

On the third Friday, Eddie and Paul and I were joined by Queenie and Harley Mike, a tentative couple, the only other guys in the building our age. After we got our hands stamped for paying the dollar-fifty cover charge, Harley Mike took us all into the alley and got us high, and Queenie brought out a pewter flask of gin to fortify our fruit juice drinks.

Loose and giggly, dancing wilder and better than I ever had before, I heard Eddie suggest we go to Spike, and the guys all froze, and said nothing at all.

Paul piped up with, "You want to take Ella to *Spike?*"

"What's Spike?" I whispered in Queenie's ear, and he said it was a leather bar, which didn't sound bad; in fact, I felt like I was dressed the part in Shane's jacket.

"But you gotta be twenty-one at Spike."

Eddie laughed his shrieky little laugh and said he knew the guy who checked IDs—no, not knew him but *knew him*, and if he let us in that night, Eddie would *know him* again.

So we all piled into my Studebaker, squealed too fast around a few corners, and ended up in a whole different world. Dark, especially in the back. The men wore leather caps and leather pants and chaps and studded dog collars, and stared with a venom that I supposed was meant to pass for some dangerous brand of sexuality.

I ordered a beer, and as I drank it I became aware that the whole place smelled of amyl nitrate, which made me groggy, and I wandered to the back to find a ladies' room, but there wasn't one. Having no special backup plan, I slumped into a corner, ended up sitting on the floor, almost invisible. As my eyes adjusted to the light I realized what it was about Spike that brought on all that silence. Rather than finding a man to take home, the men at Spike were doing it right here, in the dim booths and against the back of the bar.

Almost half of them wore leather pants that unzipped or unlaced up the back, as they allowed one huge biker or another to take a place behind them, grunting and thrusting, and reaching around in front, searching, I assumed, for assurance of their good receptions.

I tilted my bottle back and swallowed long slugs of cold beer, and wondered where the guys might have gone, but then I saw Eddie in a booth in the far corner, holding his hard penis in one hand and a strange man's head in the other, seemingly pleased with the way the two joined together.

A tall black man sat on the floor next to me, nuzzled me with his shoulder.

"What's your name, honey?"

When I told him he vaulted to his feet, laughing. "Oh my god, you're a girl. I had no idea. Honey, do you know where you are?"

I said as best I could figure I was in a butch leather bar in Hollywood, watching a bunch of guys making it in the corners in the dark. He nodded and wandered off to try again.

I nursed the feeling of the alcohol and the watching, the familiar warm buzzing energy that I stole from them, and when I wrapped my arms around myself, it made me think of Simon, holding me around the waist on the landing, telling me I shouldn't grow up to be an animal. I remembered thinking the watching was fine until he told me it wasn't. But Simon wasn't aware of my every move anymore. Just when I really started having fun Harley Mike found me and pulled me out the front door, where the guys waited on the sidewalk.

They seemed relieved to see me.

"Where the hell were you, Ella? You scared us."

Mike answered for me, saying he found me in the *back*, with great, ominous emphasis, and all mouths dropped open in grudgingly impressed disbelief.

Queenie sidled up to me and hissed in my ear, "Ella, what the hell were you doing back there?"

"Watching."

"Damn. We thought you were a nice little girl."

On the way home it was Eddie who got it in his head to go to the Rooftop Baths. "Ever been to the Rooftop? It's the only bi place in town. A hundred men to every one woman, and she's always a bow wow. One cute little girl in the whole place and she's with us. Get it? What do you think, Ella? You want to do some real watching?"

Harley Mike said, "No. She doesn't."

I said I did, and I really did, I wanted it a lot, except not that night, because of Shane's jacket, because of my solemn promise not to take it off and leave it anywhere.

And since I was near ready to pass out for the night, the idea was called until the following Friday.

When Friday came I left Shane's jacket at home with its rightful owner, and drove the four guys to the Rooftop in Atwater, where they paid my way in the door.

In the locker room we changed into towels, then slinked down dark halls lined with private rooms, most with open doors. A waiting man lounged in each one, toweled, or naked, most leaning with outstretched arms on the door frames over their heads to make their stomachs look flatter, their chests more developed.

I grabbed onto Harley Mike's towel, because he was big, and I knew that he would fight to the death to protect me. His presence formed a shield, like the chemical coating on a fire eater's tongue, and I juggled raw fire with my bare hands, because he was close by. I touched their attention and ran.

I saw only one woman, but she disappeared into a room with the man she'd come with, just the two of them, and Queenie told me that was a "ventilated" room, and when I just stared, he said there were holes in the walls of some rooms, some crotch height, some eye level, and the guys could watch, or push something in there with them, and hope it might be touched. He said most of the women who come to a place like this only tease.

We sat in the jacuzzi, and men filled it almost to overflowing and leaned against its outsides, trying to catch my eye and smiling at me with faces that said *please, please pick me. You just don't know how important it is.*

But I picked no one—the boys did the picking. They chose two young men with dark Latino looks, and nodded to them, and we strolled to a room with no "ventilation" because Harley Mike thought it would be kinder, since I had no intention of touching them, or letting them touch me, if no one knew what they got, or what they didn't.

No sooner did they step in with us than Harley Mike bolted the door from inside, and held them back with a hand on each of their bare chests, and explained in a voice difficult to challenge, "The lady prefers to just watch."

I saw their disappointment, but they stayed.

I sat in the corner as they writhed on the stained mattress, and I watched the tangled combinations of mouths and erections, and fixed balloons of nitrous oxide, the way I'd been taught, using Queenie's special "hitter," and passed them to the boys, and now and then breathed one myself. It made the world sway and dip, and contain only the dark sounds of Darth Vader breathing, and the click of wet contact, and the warm buzzing of a fire eater who doesn't feel the burn. I liked it too much. All of it, not just the drug.

The second time out the boys chose a gorgeous blond man with an attitude problem, who said that wasn't the deal he thought he'd bought himself into, and tried to pull off my towel. Harley Mike hooked a gigantic forearm around his neck, and pulled him off me, and slammed him into the back of the door. And when he came up swinging, Harley Mike hit the man so hard his head whipped around ninety degrees, and we heard a crack. Mike caught him before he could fall, and left him on the sticky mattress, his eyes struggling to focus, blood and saliva running from the corner of his mouth.

After that we got dressed to go, without talking.

In the car Harley Mike told Eddie it was a stupid idea to begin with, and he should apologize to me, but I said it was okay, he didn't have to. It was my idea as much as anybody's, because I was just so tired of pretending I could avoid growing up like my father.

Shane was out by the pool when we got home, and we sat out in the cool night, which made me feel cleaner, and he let me take hits off his cigarette. I didn't ask him why he wasn't at work, because I knew it meant that he and Jason had had a fight.

Shane said he'd heard rumors about me, that I was quite the party girl, and I mustn't let anybody talk me into anything, unless it was something I really wanted to do. He said there were a lot of good men in this place, but maybe Eddie and Paul were just kids, no offense to people my age, and maybe they just hadn't burned off all their wildness yet.

I thought maybe I hadn't either, but I didn't say so.

Jason stumbled through from the parking lot then, and we heard the car that had dropped him spin away, and he picked a drunken path to the stairs, where he clung to the railing and shot a look over his shoulder. Shane forgot to say goodbye to me before following him up.

When I got inside I found Simon sitting close to Sarah on the couch, and he excused himself without looking at me, saying he wanted to go sit by the pool. Sarah stayed inside with me, which seemed strange.

"He's worried about you," she said.

"So worried he can't even look at me?" I took a Coke out of the refrigerator and drank out of the bottle, knowing this was a lecture, and had been rehearsed.

"It's hard for Simon to talk about sex. He thought it might be better if I did."

"Nothing to talk about," I said, flopping on the couch with her. "I've never had sex. I don't plan on it."

Sarah nodded and joined Simon by the pool, and I went to bed without seeing either one of them again that night.

In the morning I told Willie everything.

"You know," she said, "you don't have to be like anyone else, even if you're related to them."

"What do you mean?" I knew what she meant.

She wore a rose corsage that day, and a red bow pulling back her hair. "Your mother has mental problems, but you don't have to. You can have a healthy view of sex, even if your father doesn't."

And then there's my sister DeeDee, I thought, and I thought of how I'd promised Simon I wouldn't follow in her footsteps. It was still a meaningless promise, though, because I couldn't remember what she'd done that I shouldn't.

"So, who do I be like?"

"Well, ideally Ella, but if you need a model for the time being, you could be a little like Simon."

"Really? What's Simon like?"

Willie suggested that I draw a portrait of Simon, not necessarily realistic, but one that would express the way I see him.

I brought it in later to show her, a curved line, a featureless silhouette, like the outline of Hitchcock before he stepped into it at the beginning of each show.

A shadow, independent of any mass that might have cast it.

How could I be more like that than I already was?

DANCING HORSE

WE WALK HALF the night, then sleep half the day. We try to set out again, but we don't get far.

The mesa rises like a dream. I guess it's about two miles away. I need to reach it, to touch it, to know for sure it's not a mirage, and won't vanish.

But as fifty miles seemed a thousand without Yozzy in my charge, or me in hers, two miles is now fifty. Yozzy stumbles, lands on her knees and, instead of righting herself, folds up underneath me.

I stand, hold her reins and ask her to her feet, but she fixes me with her bottomless dark eyes, the only liquid for miles. She says, as clearly as an old woman with a voice, *if I could go a step farther, I would have.*

I remove her hackamore and blanket, sit cross-legged on the ground and hold her head in my lap. I tell her she needs only to rest, and she tolerates the lie. She needs both rest and water, and her needs are in conflict, because water will not walk to us.

I throw the blanket across my back, extending out over my head, and I bend over her, become her awning, her shade. From the shoulders down, her body bakes in the sun—but what can I do about that? I consider covering her with my sleeping bag, but I'm afraid to seal in too much of her own body heat.

I am doing all I can.

She will rest all day, all night maybe, or even the next day, and then we will walk again. This is what I tell her.

At nightfall I decide I must find water. Even enough to fill my hat might bring her to her feet. How far I can walk, I don't know. Which way will I go? I rise and stumble slowly northeast, and a scream stops me in my tracks. It's Yozzy, calling me back. I listen to her advice, because my own ideas feel indistinct.

As I walk back I hear the shrill, restless yips of distant coyotes, so at least I know now why I mustn't leave her side. I bring her a big double handful of dry grass, but she only sniffs it and lays her head down.

The stars come out and the coyotes circle; the bright moon shows their numbers, but also their cowardice. I stand over my Yozzy, and swing the leather hackamore by its reins, and they cluster close, but run, yelping, when touched by even the air of my swing. Close up their faces are narrow and pinched, their eyes cool. They sit a handful of yards away and bark their frustration.

In the morning I sleep and Yozzy sits guard over me.

Then it's the heat of a day again, and the mesa fills my horizon, my eyes; it's close now, but not real. I can't touch it.

Yozzy's skin feels brittle, inflexible, but her eyes remain clear and dark. Knowing. Trusting. Not in me, so much. Well, maybe in me. Maybe in us.

When I close my eyes I fall into feverish delusions, in which Sam Roanhorse is wrong, Yozzy is wrong, and every element in the universe lines up at my face, against me. Then the strangest delusion of all, that the sun is gone, the sky dark, the air dark, the wind cool, and I remove the blanket to make it go away, to stop teasing me. It is not a delusion. The sky is a mass of dark clouds, the summer air painted black underneath. I look up into this beauty, feel a heavy drop hit my cheekbone and splash into my eye.

I laugh.

In the Navajo tradition, Everett taught me, there are two kinds of rain: She-rain, which mists gently down, nourishes the crops, seeps into the land, replenishes; and He-rain, which thunders away the delicate seeds, floods the washes, destroys.

The rain pours down so hard that Yozzy winces, and we laugh, though only I can be heard, at least by me. After all, Yozzy and I are not seedlings. We are old trees with deep roots. We will not wash away.

I tilt my head back and open my mouth, and as I do I cup my hands, and when they fill with rain, Yozzy licks the water away. I take off my hat, turn it upside down, and in just a moment it's half full.

I give its contents to my friend. Our gift flows into my eyes, soaks through my clothes to the skin.

Yozzy rises to her feet and shakes. She picks her way to a seam in the land, a gully, dry just moments ago, which now runs with a trickle of water. She walks her front legs down in, stands with her haunches jutting upward at an odd angle, and drinks.

She is not a beautiful horse, I realize; or rather, she wouldn't be, if she weren't the most beautiful animal in the world to me. I see her now for her true age, an ancient old woman, and I realize I have asked too much.

While she takes her fill, I drink a whole hatful of rain, and when she comes back to me again, we dance.

I swing from side to side, ignoring my stiffness, my painful feet. Ignoring all but my partner. She rears, plays games in the air with her hooves. Tosses her head in a pattern which I can see we both find pleasing.

Then I sit, as if come to my senses, and she nuzzles my ear. *You're right,* she says, *what a foolish way to spend energy,* but she expresses this without regret.

Shivering now, dripping in the downpour, eyes squinted against its fury, we walk the two miles to the mesa, side by side.

I touch it.

It's real.

THEN:

FOR THREE WEEKS prior to my eighteenth birthday, I reminded Shane every time I saw him.

"I got the night off and everything," he'd say. "You and me, kid."

The promise was that Shane would take me dancing, just the two of us, ride us to Gino's on the back of his motorcycle. Our night. It would be our night. It would make up for the eighteen years that came before it, just that one night. It had to. What else were we given?

I bleached my hair blond, like Jason did, and sliced up the knees of my jeans, and washed them until they frayed, and rolled the sleeves of the baggy white T-shirt Shane had given me.

I leaned on his motorcycle, dreaming, until almost nine-thirty, then I gave up and knocked on his door. At first I got no answer at all, but on the second knock, a muffled sound.

"Yeah?"

"Shane?"

"It's open."

He perched on the couch, leaned forward on his hands, his hair in his eyes, a cigarette between his fingers. The smoke curled over the top of his head and disappeared.

His apartment felt too bare. Pictures were missing from walls, a statue from the table. The bookcase stood empty.

On the table in front of him I saw a bottle of Scotch and a twin-edged razor blade.

He lifted his head to reveal red, swollen eyes, and took a pull from the bottle.

"Oh, Ella," he said, more disappointed in himself than I could ever be in him. "I'm sorry, Ella."

I sat with him on the couch, close, and wrapped an arm around his knee. He said Jason was gone.

"Gone gone?"

"Looks that way."

I leaned my head on his shoulder and told him not to cry.

"Your big day," he said.

"This is better than dancing, anyway." And it was, pressed up against him on the couch, making him feel better by understanding, by postponing feeling hurt until he was done hurting.

He took another drink, and I took the bottle out of his hand and had a long swallow myself, and felt the burn of it going down, the way it made my muscles loose and fuzzy, all along my arms and legs. I wrapped my arms around his waist and he held me close, with his cheek on the top of my head. His tears fell into my hair.

"Ella, don't fall in love with me," he said at last, and my stomach burned to hear the words, because I would have done anything for Shane, anything at all. Why did he have to ask the one thing I couldn't do if I tried? "Find yourself a nice straight guy, a guy who'll be all the things you want him to be." He stroked my hair, his voice mellowed with drink and pain into a sort of spoken song. "You have so much love, Ella—don't throw it away on a guy like me."

But until I met Shane I thought I had no love at all.

"Too late," I said, because it was the only thing that fit, and rang true, and my voice cracked when I said it, almost like crying, but without the help of my eyes.

He held me so tight around the ribs that I couldn't breathe all the way in, and I didn't care.

I kissed him on the mouth, and he kissed me back.

Then he stood up, and I thought he'd ask me to leave, but he took my hand and pulled me into the almost bare bedroom, and pulled off his T-shirt, and smiled in a way that made him look sadder.

He reached for my shirt and I lifted my arms for him. As he pulled it over my head, I smiled back at him. It came all the way from a place that could feel, and I thought it would break me, or that it did, and when I was still able to reach for him I was so surprised.

We just hugged each other for the longest time, with my breasts pressed up against his bare chest. He rocked me a little, like slow-dancing, and I didn't know or care if we would ever do more. I remember thinking I could die right then and it wouldn't have mattered one way or the other.

He walked me backwards to the bed, and laid me down, and I raised my hips for him; he pulled my jeans away, threw them on the floor, took off his own before he lay down on top of me with a lazy half-erection.

I could see his face in the light from the living room, his hair falling from his forehead, touching mine, and I thought, *this must be what it feels like to love someone, and if Simon feels this way for Sarah, then he should have her, and nobody should ever get in the way.*

When Shane kissed me again I tasted cigarettes and Scotch, and a trace of his sweat; and when his face brushed against mine, I felt the stubble of his whiskers burn my cheek.

I told him I loved him and he just smiled. "Big mistake," he said. Then he pushed inside me. I yelled out in pain and surprise, but I would do it all again if I could. I don't think he knew why I yelled.

He rocked me slowly, like we had all night, his eyes still swollen, his face ruined in the half-light. Every thrust brought pain and reawakened the pain of the moment before, and I never wanted him to stop, but in time he did.

He lay still with a little shudder, and as he pulled away I saw the shock on his face. I looked down to see the sheet soaked with blood.

"Oh, Ella, honey. I'm sorry. I didn't know. I thought you'd been around a little."

He brought me a wet towel, and wiped gently between my legs. As he did I kissed him and told him I wanted to do it again, but I knew we wouldn't, because he'd gone groggy and spent.

"Tell you a little secret," he said. "This was my first time too. I never did this with a girl before."

"Really? Never?"

Instead of answering, he whispered in my ear. "You saved my life tonight." Then he fell asleep or passed out in that position, half on top of me, without ever telling me how I did that.

I figured I'd ask him in the morning, but in the morning his side of the bed was empty. I woke up with the covers on the floor, Shane's leather jacket over me. When I searched the apartment for him I found only a note.

It said I should keep the jacket, because he was going home to Phoenix, where it's too hot anyway, and that I was way too good for him, and I'd figure that out some day.

I'd been to Phoenix, and I knew it got pretty cold, too, at night. I couldn't see how anybody could be too good for Shane. "Maybe that was the worst thing I could have done to you, I don't know. But if you're sorry it happened, then I'm sorry. But if you're glad, I'm glad. Look around the apartment, keep anything you can use," the note ended.

I carted home everything that belonged to Shane, his left-behind clothes, his safety razor, even the unused bar of soap from his shower. I took the rest of the bottle of Scotch.

Simon had already gone to school.

I sat home all day, didn't go to work, didn't call, drank most of the Scotch and felt nothing. I tried to remember having felt something the night before, but it seemed I must have dreamed it. Not the event, the feeling of it.

Just before Simon got home I climbed up a drainpipe onto the roof. I wore Shane's jeans, too baggy for me, damp in the crotch with leftover blood and semen, and a long, untucked T-shirt, and I stuck my head over the edge and talked to the guys down in the pool.

"You better get out of there. I'm gonna dive."

Most of them said they wouldn't do that if they were me, but we talked it out, back and forth, until Simon came home with Sarah, and as they came in from the parking lot, I took my stance.

The trick, I knew, would be to push off the roof, push away from it, hard, to propel myself out instead of straight down. If I messed up, I'd land headfirst on concrete—a detail which seemed unimportant at the time.

I stood with my toes curled over the edge and thought one more time about Shane. This time I felt it, which helped, because I knew that if I missed, at least I would never have to feel it again.

As I pushed off, Sarah screamed. And then I was freefalling, a helpless, bottomless sort of feeling, but too familiar to scare me. I closed my eyes so I wouldn't have to see how I was doing, and as my hands and face plunged into the water, I felt the tops of my feet smack the pool's edge, and scrape going in. I hit the heels of my hands on the opposite wall of the pool, then surfaced to shouts and cheers and Simon with no blood at all in his face, and eyes cold and angry.

I pushed up and climbed out of the pool. Simon grabbed me by the wrist and pulled me inside, slamming the patio door behind us. Sarah stood frozen, looking unsure of her next move.

"What in god's name did you think you were doing, Ella? You could have been killed!" It was the loudest I'd heard him yell since the disposable-lighter incident.

"But it worked out fine, Simon." As I said it, I followed his eyes down my body, and saw the tops of my feet bleeding and swollen, the thin red blood mixing with the pool water I dripped into the carpet.

He stepped in close to me, his voice deep. "You could have broken your neck. You could have crippled yourself. Don't I have enough trouble taking care of you now?"

As I walked for the door, I heard him call after me that he didn't mean that, that it came out wrong, that he was only scared for me, and I needed to come back so we could talk. I slammed the door behind me.

I walked back up to Shane's apartment, where I thought I could still smell him, and sat on his couch, just the way he had the night before. On the table before me I saw the only pieces of Shane I'd forgotten to claim—a half-empty pack of Kools and the double-edged razor blade.

I lit a cigarette, which made me dizzy, trying to smoke the whole thing by myself. When I picked up the razor blade, I heard Shane in my head, saying *you saved my life tonight.*

I stared for a long time at the inside of my wrist, the little section just below the scraped heel of my hand, which was normal skin, just above the scar line. The tighter I clenched my fist, the clearer I saw the little blue veins.

I touched it with the corner of the blade, so sharp I felt nothing as it bit a short slice. I saw a well of bright blood collect and drop onto the floor, and I screamed. But not for myself.

I screamed for DeeDee. And I knew then what I wasn't supposed to do.

I found a washcloth in the cupboard, and held it to try to stop the bleeding. Then I used Shane's phone to call Willie. I asked her if I could come over.

She said she'd never heard me so upset, and offered to come to me, but I needed to stay away from Simon for a while. I drove to her house.

She met me in the driveway, in sweatpants and her good blouse from work, and she looked at my wet hair and clothes, my bare, bleeding feet, my scraped palms, the bloody washcloth on my wrist, and didn't even ask questions.

I fell up against her and she held me, and I sobbed and heaved, and I tried hard to make tears come out, but they wouldn't move. I wanted to use an ax to break into the place where they lay hiding. I wanted to free all the prisoners.

"Willie," I whispered, "DeeDee killed herself."

And she held me, and rocked me, and said, "I know, Ella. I know."

SIMON'S HOUSE

THE SKY CLEARS, but my clothes still drip, and the day turns to dusk. With the sheer stone wall of the mesa against my back, I climb onto Yozzy, and as we stand, considering our options, three long-eared jackrabbits break out of nowhere and head east.

So we do the same, only more slowly. I fear the cold that will come with night, with a wet sleeping bag, in wet clothes, on wet ground.

I think only of this, and how far we will ride.

The world has dropped out from under me. Why did I allow myself to see the touching of the mesa as a journey's end? The mesa is miles long, maybe longer than we traveled to get here. How far will we ride it, until we find what we're looking for, or until we don't?

And somehow, one way or the other, we must go back.

I pull the damp paper package from my sleeping bag and chew on a sheet of beef jerky, and think of Everett and May. They would have a fire tonight, and a hot bath. A hot dinner. Why would anything in the universe envy me?

And then, in the murky dusk, Yozzy stops suddenly, and I fall forward against her neck. In front of her feet, I see a circle of three jackrabbits. If she moved into the circle, surely she would disperse them, but she won't.

She takes a step backward, then pivots sideways. She repeats this process three times. Then, facing the mesa, she waits patiently until I see it.

The cave entrance is puddled with leftover moisture. The fire pit is flooded with water and ash; it has a spit on forked sticks. It is not a tent, as in Everett's dream. There is no animal skin across the door, as in mine. No animal skin anywhere. Sam was the best dreamer, so far as I can tell, in that he has provided no inaccurate details. And Sam said Simon was home.

I wonder if my heart is beating.

I sit straight on Yozzy's back, cup my hands to my mouth and shout *Simon.* In my peripheral vision, I watch the jackrabbits scatter. The mesa echoes it back to me, but when the sound fades, nothing rises to take its place.

I am a better dreamer than I thought.

I slide down, scramble up the rock to the plateau facing his door. Now my heart is beating, I know. I hear it, and feel it. I wade through the puddle to the mouth of his cave. I call his name again.

I step inside. The entryway bends, and it's dark further in. I trip over something and fall onto the heels of my hands, scraping them. I lie still until my eyes adjust to the light, and I see I've tripped over one of a pair of five-gallon plastic water bottles. It's nearly half full.

I look and feel further around, until I'm satisfied with the dimensions of the cave. It's just a hollow. A hole in the rock. The broadest expanse of floor is covered by a pair of faded overalls.

There is nothing else to be seen. No hunting rifle. No big knife. No Simon, alive or dead.

And yet I can honestly say I've found Simon's house.

I lift the half-full plastic bottle to carry it outside for Yozzy, and as I do, I see several boxes of ammunition hidden between bottle and wall, and a flat, black object. I pick it up and carry it out into the half-light.

A wallet. I hold it in my hand. I want to open it, but I'm afraid. *Do you hear that, Simon? I'm afraid, and I know it.* As I try, my hands shake, and I drop it onto the red-brown, dirt-coated rock. When I bend to retrieve it, it's open.

I see a row of credit cards peeking from their separate slots. I grasp the top of a gas company card and pull it out into my hand, holding it under my nose, straining to read it.

It says *Simon Peter Ginsberg.*

When I'm done reading, still half unsure of my vision, I touch the raised letters and read them again, with my fingers. It says the same. I return the card to its slot, open the money compartment, and find five bills, at least three of which are twenties.

I slip the wallet into my wet jeans pocket.

Maybe I have found Simon. Maybe he's around the corner urinating, fetching water, watching the stars come out. Maybe he's long gone, but considerate enough to pay my way home.

I go back for the water bottle, pour for Yozzy into my muddy, battered hat. She drinks two hatfuls.

I remove her blanket and hackamore, and she wanders a hundred yards away, to the thickest scrub, to nibble.

Knowing she is satisfied, I tip the bottle back and drink, water spilling down my chin, soaking my already soaked clothes. I watch her graze in the dark, watch the moon rise, and it smiles at me. It says, *nobody knows. Some things no one can tell you.*

I realize then how far I have come. How much I have accomplished. I have done the impossible. I have defied death and probability. What remains is out of my control.

It's also the only part that matters.

I sleep on Simon's bed, on the dry overalls, the dry cave floor, sheltered from the wind. I dream about madness.

In the morning I am still in Simon's house alone.

THEN:

I DROVE SIMON and Sarah to the airport in Simon's Oldsmobile, soon to become my own.

"I'll call you every day," he said.

"You don't have to call every day, Simon."

"Well, at first. And you can call collect, anytime. Day or night."

"I don't have to call collect, Simon. I work two full-time jobs. I'll be all right."

He hugged me, which I know was hard for him, and Sarah hugged me, and whispered that I could always change my mind. When they stepped onto the plane, terror mixed with relief. It had been so hard to watch them go through all that. Was this really what I inspired in those around me?

Simon and I had moved shortly after the Shane incident, into both halves of a tiny duplex on Silver Lake Boulevard, not a mile from Willie's house.

He married Sarah at city hall, downtown. They honeymooned at a Malibu hotel for the weekend. They lived in one side of the duplex, I lived in the other, quietly, without expectation, allowing each day to look and feel much like the one before.

Simon quit school to work a second job, and when he announced his plan to move to Sacramento, where Sarah's father had offered him a job with his investment firm, he seemed to take for granted that I would come along.

That I would even need to think it over sent him into an uncharacteristic snit.

"Ever since you met Shane you don't need me anymore."

He looked embarrassed the moment his words hit the floor, lying like an animal needlessly killed.

I left for my own apartment. If only Shane were the issue, I would need Simon again. Apart from a postcard, though, forwarded from our old Hollywood address, Shane was gone.

I rose at five forty-five to join Willie on her morning walk around the reservoir. This was nothing special. I did it every day.

"Why do they even call this a lake?" I said, my voice carping and cool. I pointed to the barbed wire strands which topped the chain-link fence, the steep concrete of its sides. "I mean, have we been living in the city too long, or what?"

"What's on your mind, Ella?" She wore a red bandanna tying back her unruly hair, no makeup—her usual morning outfit. She had proven, with that simple question, why Simon was wrong to say I could get a new counselor in the new city. Maybe he could just leave Sarah, marry a new wife once he settled in.

"Simon's going to move to Sacramento."

"Oh. That's a pretty big something."

"I guess."

"Are you going to move with him?"

"He wants me to."

"Do you want to?"

"No."

We walked in silence, to the far end of the reservoir, around the bend, back toward home, keeping up the brisk pace that Willie liked.

"He's not Simon anymore," I said on the home stretch. "I still remember when he was. But what good does that do?"

"But you still love him?"

"Well, yeah, but it just doesn't make that much difference if he's there or if he's not. He's gone either way, you know? It's because of me. You know that, don't you?"

"What is?"

"This thing about Simon not being Simon. He's doing that for me."

"Care to elaborate on that?"

"Doesn't matter now. He's going."

She had said it sounded like I'd made up my mind.

I watched their plane taxi down the runway, but I turned to leave for work before the wheels lifted off.

He called in the morning, but what was there to say?

For three weeks running I followed a careful routine. Morning walks with Willie, work, sleep. Laundromat on Sunday, grocery shopping Thursday afternoon. On the days I worked only one shift, I caught up on my sleep.

Everything went fine until a holiday forced a day off. I loved to work. Life was always in perfect order, from the beginning of a shift to the end of it. This life held what my other life so painfully lacked. A rule book. An order of moments. Show up. Count the cash drawer. Initial the register tape. Sign in. Smile at the customer. Ring up the customer. Give correct change. If there's no customer, wipe the glass on the refrigerator cases.

In time of any doubt, ask the boss, and he'll differentiate right from wrong.

I probably could have survived on just one of those jobs. Financially, that is.

On Presidents' Day the bank was closed, and it fell on my day off at the market. I woke in the morning without a plan. I lay on my back on the couch for most of the day. Called Willie at work, but she was busy with a patient.

I filled the Oldsmobile's tank, drove to Santa Monica, watched the waves come in by the last light. *They have no plan,* I told myself, *but they keep busy all day long, just doing the same thing over and over. They ask no questions.* I told myself that maybe I ask too many questions. I drove back through Topanga Canyon, wove through Coldwater Canyon, Laurel Canyon, watched the lights glow inside each of the houses, looking warm. Something warm existed in each of those homes. For a split second I almost thought back to Mrs. Hurley, but I stopped myself before it had gone too far.

I cut through Hollywood, drove up into Griffith Park, circling the observatory parking lot until I found a space. I made it through the door into the telescope area just moments before closing time.

Virgil seemed glad to see me.

"Ella. How've you been? Haven't seen you in ages. Where's Simon?"

The question surprised me, as though I thought he should know. Everybody should know.

"He moved away."

"Really?" I heard all the questions he didn't ask, and it was just as well. It took some hunting on his part, I know, to find one that might sound properly supportive. "So, how does it feel to be on your own?"

I shrugged, my gaze fixed on a chart of the solar system. "All right, I guess. Until today. I don't have anything to do today."

I thought about seeing Willie, just ducking out right then, and finding her at home, because it was important, what I needed to say, to know, and I knew Willie so much better. But my feet stayed stuck, and I realized I hadn't sought Virgil by whim or accident.

"Well," he said. "You're here, that's something to do. Come on. You want to look at the moon?"

"But you're closed, aren't you?"

"Not to you."

I pressed my eye to the lens, and saw the moon dead full. I saw mountains and valleys and craters.

"Where is he?" I said.

"Who?"

"The man in the moon." I'd never seen a full moon through the telescope, and I always thought if I did, I'd see him.

"Well, you get closer up, it kind of ruins the illusion."

Without realizing I was going to, I told Virgil about my resentful disappointment on the night of the moon landing. He listened well—one of Virgil's steadfast traits.

Then he said, "You know, I felt that way, too, just a little. And I couldn't have been more surprised. Here I am, a scientist. But I guess part of me is still a mystic. Or just a dreamer. It always seemed so ethereal. Tell anyone and I'll deny it."

I smiled and pressed my eye to the lens again, because it was easier and safer to talk that way.

"Simon wants to be an investment broker."

"Okay." I could tell by the way he said it that he wouldn't state his feelings on the subject until I'd stated mine.

"Is that a good thing to be, Virgil?"

"Well, it depends. Anything's a good thing to be if that's what you want."

Now, I felt, we were nearing the heart of the issue.

"How do you know what you want?"

Virgil scratched his chin, the way he always did when thinking. It made him look more like a scientist.

"I guess you just go by what you feel."

"Damn!" I shot it out hard, full of disappointment. Wouldn't you know it would come down to that? So what about me— how would I ever know?

"What's the matter, Ella?"

I didn't dare say what I was thinking. I wanted Virgil to be pleased with me, happy and surprised at how I turned out. No talking to DeeDee, or letting on that I couldn't feel. Even Simon didn't know that.

"Well, it's just that . . . he was going to be an astronomer."

"I know, Ella. I remember. But maybe that was just a child-hood dream."

My mouth fell open, my eyes came up to meet his, and I know I didn't hide my amazement. I forgot to even try. A childhood dream? There are dreams for children and others for grownups? My god, how far behind had I already fallen?

"I never had a dream, Virgil. Ever. I never wanted to be any-thing. Just happy."

Virgil smiled. "That's all any of us want to be, is happy, Ella, that's all a dream is. It's just an idea of what will get you to happy."

His face took on a helpless, sympathetic look. This was an ex-change in a foreign language to me. I guess it showed.

I said, "I never had a single idea of how to get to happy. I guess that's why I never did."

"What are you, seventeen, eighteen years old?"

"Nineteen."

"It takes most of us a little longer than nineteen years. It takes some all their lives."

I realized then what it was, what chewed at me, like mice in a dark corner of the cellar, but I never once said it out loud. I only ever had one dream, once, in my whole life, and it was to make Simon happy. And I worked hard for it, too. Sent him back to school to find it, but he picked up and walked away. Didn't Simon want to be happy? I wanted it badly for him—couldn't some of that rub off?

As if Virgil read my mind, he said, "There are a lot more easy opportunities in investments than in astronomy."

I asked what *easy* had to do with anything, but he didn't answer.

Just before I left, he said he was surprised, pleasantly surprised, to see me again, to see how I grew up. He couldn't quite find the words to say more.

If he could have spoken the truth, without fear of hurting me, I think he would have said he was surprised I grew up at all.

People could have said things like that in front of me. I liked the truth, if I ever heard it. But no one ever did.

No one except Shane, and Shane was gone.

EYES OF THE WILD MAN

AS I STEP out into the cool morning, Yozzy wanders up to greet me, and I offer her a hatful of water, which she gratefully accepts. I wish I had more to give her, or to give myself, but we have drunk almost all the water already.

I have two pieces of beef jerky left. I chew on one slowly, remembering the warm faces of Everett and May.

It's about six-thirty, I'm guessing, which means five-thirty in California, and I wonder if Willie is out, walking briskly around the concrete lake. And I wonder, *is she thinking about me now? Someone has to think about me now.*

The sky is empty, the landscape empty. I slip back inside Simon's house, into cool shade, and it's empty. Tears come, and I let them, comforted by the flow of them on my cheeks, like company.

Did I really come all this way to find emptiness, which I held in such a vast supply at home?

I will not leave until I know.

Hours later the moon comes out, before dusk, and it asks, *what if you never know? What if your question has no answer?*

I hear Yozzy's hooves against the stone; she asks for more water. I give her the last, though I'm thirsty. I eat the last piece of beef.

I look to the moon, who smiles and says, *if you need to find even more emptiness, you could always die here yourself.*

I decline.

I look around for Yozzy, but she's out on the open plain, seeking better grazing. I pick up her hackamore and blanket, throw my bedroll on my shoulder. Will she be relieved when I tell her we're going home? Or will she be disappointed in me, and will I see that in the depth of her dark, liquid eye?

I never learn.

As I cup my hands to call her name, I see a shadow, east against the mesa. Fear grips me, running along my belly like river water. It never occurs to me it might be Simon, which is as it should be, because then, as he comes closer, I feel no disappointment.

I dive back inside Simon's house, but that's a mistake, because surely he is coming this way. Whoever he is, I am in his house. Whoever he is, he is not Simon.

I watch him from the sheltered darkness. He is a wild man. A white man, but not one of us. His hair, thick and tangled, shines white and fine in the dying sun, his unmanageable beard just slightly darker. An older man, but strong enough to be danger-ous. He comes close, to Simon's fire pit, and I'm trapped inside his house.

He carries a rifle and drags the gutted carcass of a deer. His eyes appear gray in the slant of light. He wears dirty underwear and a tattered blanket thrown as a cape across his shoulders.

He leaves the carcass in the dirt, and I see he also drags a bur-lap sack filled with gnarled pieces of fallen branches, which he lays on the ground in a careful order. He must have traveled far, I think, for a bag of wood like this.

He works methodically, shoveling handfuls of dirt into the fire pit to form a new, drier floor.

He pulls a long hunting knife from its sheath, hidden some-where beneath his cape, and shaves thick curls of kindling from a soft branch.

He is faced partly away from me, and as I watch his profile, he moves with a certain grace, but it's an angry grace, I think, a grace I might not have recognized yesterday, or the day before. Then I realize I am looking at my brother Simon's killer. What else can he be? He is not Simon, but he has Simon's wallet. Or he did. He is not Simon, but I followed him from the spot of Simon's ordeal.

I wonder: Is my mission only to kill the man who killed my brother? Or to bring him to justice, to bring Sarah her answer, so she can wear black, and start slowly over? So that I can sleep, and return to marginal sanity, knowing I have done the only thing left worth doing?

If so, I hope it brings something more than emptiness. His rifle leans against the stone wall of the mesa, and I know I must take him now, win or lose. I must use my only weapon: surprise. I must not let him corner me here.

I can't get to the rifle, not without going through him. I wait, I watch, I feel my time run down. I wonder with a chill if he'll see Yozzy. If he'll try to catch her. Or shoot her. I wonder: If I die, will she be brave enough and accepting enough to go home without me?

If she does, Everett will say a prayer for me. I could do worse. I'm scared, but I'm not sorry I came. I will die with dignity, or I'll win. Yozzy would have no preference, but then, Yozzy is a horse, for which I envy her.

He lays the knife down, bends over the fire pit, and I launch myself into flight. I have only one smooth movement left to my life, unless I do this exactly right. My hand grazes the knife but misses, and I can't afford to stop. I hit his back with all my weight, send him sprawling hard across his half-laid firewood, and as I land on his back, I hear the wind escape him. This gives me a split second to untangle myself, struggling for breath, and I return for the knife.

He rolls onto his back, and I land on his belly, and press the point of the knife to his throat until the skin dimples lightly. I do not draw blood.

I feel a stiff pain in my gut, because I wanted to see Simon's eyes, even though I knew it could not be Simon. I wanted it to be, when I got closer, but, like looking at the moon through Virgil's telescope, the closeness further destroys the illusion.

These hard gray eyes do not belong to my brother, and so must belong to his killer.

He tries to draw a breath, to release a sound, but I stop him with a hiss that scares even me. I am wild enough to match him.

Though it's an odd time to care, I realize I haven't seen myself in a mirror in weeks, and I wonder how I look to this wild man, this killer. Maybe I look more vicious than he. Maybe I am.

"I might kill you," I say, in a scratchy whisper. "Even if you hold still I might kill you, so definitely don't move."

As I hear myself say it, I think I'm an actress, buying his compliance with a lie. I will not kill him, except to save my life, but I have a right to lean on his ignorance of my nature. Then I think of him as my brother's killer and I wonder: Would I?

"What have you done with my brother Simon?"

The words echo loud, the cry of a warrior. At the corner of my eye I see Yozzy's head snap up.

My prisoner utters a strange sound, a barely human sound, but questioning, in a universal tone.

I hold the flat, sharp edge of the knife along his carotid artery. I could. I might.

"Simon. My brother Simon. You had his wallet. Where did you get it? What did you do to him? Talk. Now."

He utters a sound, but I can't make it out. Maybe he doesn't speak English. Maybe he is truly wild, raised by wolves. Maybe his father was a coyote, and by night he stalked me, and tried to take Yozzy away. Maybe the moon is right, and my question has no answer. Maybe I came all this way to learn only that.

I become aware of myself, sitting on his chest, and I want to pull away. But if I do, I give him an opening, a chance at the upper hand.

"I can't understand you. Do you speak English?"

He nods slightly. I'm not giving him much room for expression in the way I hold his knife.

"Then say it. Where is my brother Simon? What did you do to him?"

His eyes change. They broaden and soften, into some semblance of humanity, and I feel a wave of gooseflesh along my arms, and a buzzing tremble all down my belly, in the place that knows things it will not say. The place I try to break with an ax, to free my tears, but they must become thin to slip through the walls.

I think of a song from Jewish religious school. *So high, you can't get over it, so low, you can't get under it, so wide, you can't get around it.*

I shake the words away again.

I want to cry, right now. For my brother Simon, and for myself, and somehow, inexplicably, for my sorry prisoner. But I can't let him see me cry if I'm about to kill him, and it's not completely out of the question.

He looks into my eyes, and I'm afraid he'll see the chink of my emotion, but before I turn my face away, I see that he is crying. Big, heavy tears that roll away from the far corners of his eyes, and his mouth twists like a child's, showing the cracks in his life, in this moment.

He says something. I sense it's in English, because I think I make out one word. It sounds like, "Sorry."

"What?" I shout. "I can't hear you." I won't lighten up on him. I won't feel sorry for him. I can't. I didn't come all this way to love my brother's murderer.

That feeling returns, rippling the skin on my arms and belly. I don't want to kill this man, I don't want to hate him, but if I came all this way, lived through all this to learn a bond with Simon's killer, then I don't want the lesson. I'd sooner hand him the knife.

And now he knows it. We touch a moment in time when if I am to kill him I must do it now, and if I am not to kill him, then the balance of power shifts back to him. I cannot arrest him. I cannot bring him all the way to justice from here. The arm of the law is not that long. And I am not the law.

He jerks underneath me, aware of the perfect moment to unbalance me. In fact, he has already unbalanced me, by proving I won't cut his throat. And now he performs a sudden, literal version of the insult, and performs it well. I fall away from him, he stumbles backwards over the fire pit, falls sprawling and tumbling on his back along the rocks to the plain. The knife flies out of my hand, I can't see where to. He scrambles to his feet and runs away.

I still have his gun.

I pick it up and aim at him, and follow him through his own rifle sight, running away, claiming victory. *I have taken your brother Simon and now I will take your opportunity for revenge, the kind that lets you sleep at night. Unless you pull the trigger.*

But he's nearly out of range now, and I am not a sharpshooter. I am not a cowboy or a Navajo. I've never held a gun before. It's too late.

As I lower the rifle scope I see Yozzy, head up, watching me at some distance, chewing grass, her jaw working, her eyes following only me. Not the running figure. Me. I set the rifle down on the red dirt of the mesa and she returns her attention to the scrubby grass.

She's right, of course. We did not come all this way for revenge.

THEN:

ABOUT A WEEK before my thirty-third birthday, he woke me out of a sound sleep with his phone call. I thought it was Simon. It almost always was.

Instead, a voice I hadn't heard for more than twelve years, and didn't recognize, even when he told me his name. I'd never spoken to him on the phone before; I supposed that was why.

"I'll bet you don't even remember me."

"Shane, that's the dumbest thing you ever said to me."

"Okay."

They say you always remember your first, but to further complicate the situation, he was my only. Still, after all that time.

"How did you find me?"

"From information. How many Ella Ginsbergs you think are listed?"

"Where are you?"

"Not far."

He warned me in advance that he wasn't traveling alone. If he came by, he'd have to bring his friend Raphael. I didn't mind. The fact that Raphael was smart enough to love Shane didn't preclude our getting along.

He also warned me that he didn't look the same.

I opened my front door and there they were, two strangers. One rugged, dark and handsome—but not Shane—one pale, emaciated, eyes gray and sunken—maybe Shane, but only because one of them had to be.

What could be so strong, I wondered, so much stronger than a vital human body, to bring such change, to replace health and good humor with an image of itself? To cause me to look into the eyes of a man and see only disease, not the host of the man.

Raphael held Shane's arm and helped him in, helped him sit down in a soft overstuffed chair.

"Where do you live now?" I asked him, and he exchanged a look with Raphael. I knew he had come with an agenda, a sort of desperation. In fact, I'd known it on the phone. Sometimes, at the very bottom of our lives, we must ask ourselves, isn't there some fool who used to love me?

"We're sort of homeless," he said. "I'm too sick to work. Raphael lost his job in Phoenix because they found out I was sick."

Then I knew what was so strong.

I jumped up from my seat on the couch, and Raphael jumped up, defensive, as if about to be shown the door, which I suppose he was used to. I threw the couch cushions in all directions, and drew out the folding bed, and told Shane he was in no shape to be up, and if he held on for a minute, I'd get him some sheets.

Raphael got a job in this new place where no one knew them, and we pooled our resources to buy more sheets, about ten sets more over the following week, so we could change Shane's bed three or four times a day.

Raphael did all the laundry, changed the bedding by himself when Shane grew too sick to get up and sit elsewhere, and took the brunt of the ugly work with cheer. It was accepted that I did poorly around sickness; it was never judged or questioned. The attitude prevailed that I was doing enough.

I did the easy things, held his hand and read him bedtime stories, John Irving and J.D. Salinger and Anaïs Nin. And the night he rocked with a coughing fit that wanted to tear his body apart from itself, I threw my arms around him to hold him together. When he fell quiet I told him I loved him, and he laughed.

"Big mistake," he said, so quietly I almost didn't hear.

By morning he'd fallen into a coma, and we called an ambulance to take him to County Hospital. I dropped by after work to hold his hand and read him bedtime stories. John Irving. J.D. Salinger. Anaïs Nin.

Only for a couple of days.

When Shane was dead, Raphael gathered a bereavement group—one that had never existed before—with a handwritten note on the hospital bulletin board. We gathered at my house, and he and I held hands all through it, every Tuesday and Thursday night, feeling lucky that we had each other, someone else who mourned our identical loss.

We held each other on the couch for long hours afterwards, and when the hugging tried to deepen out, to become more, I reminded him that he still hadn't been tested. This made him quiet, and killed the mood.

More than two months passed before I managed to pack him into my run-down Oldsmobile and drive him to the health department, where they made him wait three silent, drawn days for his test results.

When he came out of that room, I didn't ask. I could tell.

He talked about it in the group that night, and learned he wasn't the only one, not even close, and then Raphael and Ed and Jonathan and Jamey and David and Mark and Carey learned to mourn themselves, while they were at it. Funny how much harder that is.

Raphael had a photo of Shane, taken in the last days, and he kept it in the corner of the mirror. When he moved to his own apartment, I asked him to please take it away.

I preferred to remember Shane in the stream of light from the living room, his hair falling onto my forehead. Every day that he had lived with me, I searched for some verification of that old him, but the old was gone.

Sometime in 1989 my Oldsmobile got stolen, which was no great loss, but that old leather jacket had been left behind the seat, and that was.

So much for living in the past.

BREAKING BREAD

I HAVE HIS gun, his knife, his water bottles, his evening kill. I have his home. For the moment that is everything I've been needing. I find some satisfaction in that. I have not been left completely empty-handed; even as he has taken from me, I have forced him to give some small concession in return.

I finish the fire he started, restacking the branches, scattered when I attacked him, resetting the spit and its stick braces, which we knocked away. Before undergoing the tedious process of rubbing two sticks together, I search the cave and find three boxes of wooden matches stuffed into an old ammunition case.

With the fire going well, I unsheathe the knife again, and attempt to sever and skin a haunch of the deer. It's a grisly process, and I stand outside myself as I do it, knowing I might not have been capable of the act last week, or last night.

I think about another deer, one I found once on the highway, on my way to Sacramento to visit Simon. She'd been hit, paralyzed at some low point on her spine, and I stopped and helped carry her back half off the highway. A passing motorist told me not to touch her, she'd hurt me. She bled on me, but she didn't hurt me.

A man from Fish and Game came out and shot her through the ear. It was fast and clean.

On my next trip I stopped and tried to salvage her skull, but the animals had carried most everything away.

I force my mind back to the present, against its will.

I wonder what I must look like by now. I know I'm filthy, but I'd like to see my own eyes, to see if I look wild, like Simon's killer, and if I'd know myself apart from him.

I look down at the skin, still slightly bloody, draped across my knees, and I realize that now almost everything any of us dreamed is here. The cave, the deerskin, the fire. Everything but Simon. I throw the skin down below.

I'm not sure what to do with the balance of the carcass. I can't eat it all, and I can't stop thinking of it as a mutilated corpse. I can't pretend I don't know it will draw the coyotes. But I can't throw it off the bluff. It's too heavy. So I do something I can't imagine I would do. Maybe I do it to prove I'm stronger every minute than I was the minute before. I cut the head off the deer with the wild man's knife. I can't cut through the bone. I have to snap it. The neck bone gives way with a sickening crack. I throw the head to the dirt beneath me. Maybe the coyotes will take it and go away. Maybe it will be enough for them. If not, there's more. I control dinner—mine and theirs. I can even control a coyote.

I press the sharpened end of the spit through the thickest curve of venison, thread it through like a needle. I set it into the cradle of its holder, hoping dinner will somehow ease the fact that I have failed to find my brother Simon and bring him home.

I sit with the rifle across my knees. I'm strong enough now to hold it and keep it, to use it to protect my horse and to protect myself. We are all that matters now. We are all we have left. I hope we will prove to be enough.

Just to be sure we will be, I go into the cave, bring out five cartridges, and teach myself to load and fire the gun. The shots fly up into the still air, maybe come down somewhere. I don't know. I just know I can shoot if I have to.

I stare out onto Yozzy's grazing land, which is intermittently obscured by rising smoke. Fat and meat juices begin to drip, causing flashes of grease fire, causing sparks, like little angels, or devils, splitting like atoms, maybe into some of each.

The dusk comes to settle. It's a strange sense of peace.

Then the haunch of my dinner drops off into the flames, because I only pretend to know how to cook a haunch of deer at an open fire. Because the outer layer has cooked, and only the outer layer was threaded onto the spit. I try to brush off the dirt and ash, but it's too hot to touch. I burn my hand pulling it out of the pit.

I sit quiet and hungry while it cools, watching coyotes line up in the distance. Watching them gather, shift, sit, stare. Sniff. I know they smell my dinner, but between the devils and my dinner is my horse, and I know I'll have to do something about that. I jump down to the dirt below, not realizing how much it will hurt until I land on my feet. I take the rifle with me to fetch Yozzy.

The coyotes react to my presence, my approach. They jump, circle and sit a few feet further back. Angry at their refusal to scatter, to run from me outright, I raise the rifle scope to my eye and aim at them. This they seem to understand.

I watch their haunches and tails rise and fall as they lope off into the night. I feel better now. I need to inspire fear in the devils. I need to be at least that strong.

I lead Yozzy with one hand against her neck, and she picks her way onto the rock at a low place I indicate. I have found a place where she can climb up onto the base of the stone mesa. It's probably not good for her, to spend the night on rock. But to spend the night out in an unprotected open space with those hungry devils—the rock couldn't hurt her more than that.

The coyotes move close again, mill beneath us in a kind of slow motion. They respect my weapon, but also their own skill and resources. Stealthy and hungry and smart enough to be frightening. Sleep will be out of the question.

We pick our way back to the fire.

I go in after my sleeping bag, open it out and spread it on the rock, in case she needs to collapse. As she has been prone to do lately. She steps onto it, sinks to her knees and lies like a foal, her legs tucked underneath her. I sit on the edge of the bag, lean back against her barrel.

The meat has cooled sufficiently, so I thread the spit through much deeper this time, almost to the bone. The rough stick scrapes my palm, and the pressure needed for the task makes my hand ache. But I am able to set my dinner back over the fire to cook. My hands are smeared with charcoal and dirt. I wipe them on my jeans.

I need this dinner.

I wish I could offer Yozzy part of it, share my hot meal with her. But a horse has no use for a deer haunch. I feel the warmth of her barrel against my back. I wish I could graze on scrubby grass and grow strong enough to travel home. I envy her that.

I wonder if she is disappointed because we failed. She doesn't feel disappointed where we press together.

I've never eaten venison before. The outer layer is burned and gritty, but I like it. The inside is raw; I'll have to set it on the spit again when I've eaten what little is cooked. I try not to think of the color of the raw meat when I skinned it, or the sound of the neck bone cracking.

As I eat, I think about the ritual of apologizing to the soul of the animal, as I've read that Native Americans do. It strikes me as a form of grace. Saying grace. Or just being grace. I am still on the Navajo Nation, wishing Navajo grace traveled with me on this land, or that Everett had packed some with my dried beef. But I don't go so far as to complete the ritual. I say a word or two of apology out loud, but my voice only reminds me that I am not a Navajo. Just a temporary squatter on this land. Everett would just have to understand.

I hear the growling of coyotes, fighting over the deer's head and skin below.

When I've eaten my meal to the bone, I throw the leftovers down, like a ransom. *This is what you came for, now go.* Taking their prizes, the dark animals run off into the night.

I say to Yozzy, "We drank the last of the water. I'm sorry."

She seems unconcerned. We are rested, watered, fed. We are armed against our enemies, coyote and human. We have water bottles. And a strong rain has come through to replenish the land. There is water within our reach. We only have to reach for it.

I can't sleep anyway, until the coyotes leave with the sunlight. And night is the time for any kind of travel. Even a white woman from the city knows that.

I cut off a strap of the wild man's overall bedding, with my own knife, Earl's knife. The one I've owned for twenty-five years. I use the strap to lash the necks of the two bottles together. I keep the rifle with me at all times. I am that unsure. I load my jeans pocket with cartridges before setting off.

Yozzy stands when she sees I'm ready to go.

I throw the blanket across Yozzy's back, set the bottles on either side of her withers. We pick our way across the rocks, and I let her climb down alone, and she circles back to allow me to ease off the plateau onto her, and we ride east.

We find a wash in the moonlight, though we ride far to reach it. It's marked by a ribbon of trees, and tall, live vegetation. Yozzy walks out into the running coolness, dips her head to drink.

I slip down, remove my boots, tie them together, stuff my socks inside and sling them across her back, and she holds them for me. My feet are bare, unbandaged, cold, partly healed. I squat, like Everett, rifle across my knees, and drink from my hands. Maybe I can fool the land into thinking I belong here. Maybe if I look and act strong enough, Yozzy and I will make it home.

I fill the bottles half full in the shallow wash and set them on the bank, and sit beside them with my feet in the cool flow, and watch Yozzy graze on real grass. I know the dry scrub she's subsisted on is low in nutrition. I have often wished I had more to offer her. Now I do.

I want to ride back now because I'm afraid the wild man will come. I want to jump onto Yozzy's back and ask her to find Sam Roanhorse's house again. I hope she can, because I doubt I can. And now that Simon's survival is no longer at issue, I feel more concerned with my own. It makes me want to move, to act.

But I can't bring myself to begrudge Yozzy her first good meal in days. My belly is full and warm, and I owe her no less.

I watch Yozzy graze until sunrise.

THEN:

FOUR AND A HALF months before his disappearance, my brother Simon came to visit me on short notice, as always. I never minded. We ordered a pizza, then sat out on the front stoop of my courtyard apartment, staring up at the sky, or down the steep, landscaped stairs to the street.

He took a flask of tequila from his pocket, opened it and offered it to me. I shook my head.

"Gives me a headache."

That wasn't the reason. It did give me a headache, but if it had also given me a feeling I enjoyed, I don't suppose I would have minded. The truth was I felt quite uncentered enough on my own, with no outside assistance. And watching Simon's gradual progression into that bottle made me just as sick. Which I didn't say. It was his life.

As he held it out, I noticed that all of his fingernails were bitten deeply past the quick, and the skin around them looked swollen and sore.

He recapped the flask, then broke out the harmonica, as always. The one Mrs. Hurley had given him for his eighteenth birthday. The one that used to belong to her freeman grandfather.

"Do you remember those cookies she used to make for your school lunch?"

"Will you stop, Simon?"

His words brought me a familiar queasiness. Of course I remembered, as soon as it was mentioned. Nothing from that time lay buried too deeply.

Much as I loved his visits, Simon had a bad habit of getting drunk and talking about Mrs. Hurley.

"Look, you're thirty-six years old, Ella. Don't you think it's time you could remember something as simple as a cookie?"

Simon's reference involved a big sugar cookie she baked when she felt particularly cheery, which was mostly postbrandy each evening. Sometimes, when packing my school lunch, she'd use an icing tube to write, "Hi, Ella," on its big, flat face, in red gel icing that hardened, and didn't smear when she wrapped it.

In my paranoia, I always wondered if the other Columbus schoolkids stared at me, and thought I should be happier, friendlier, better, coming from such obviously ideal surroundings.

I said, "I don't see what age has to do with this."

He snorted his disgust, played "Red River Valley," filtering bent notes through the echo chamber of his hand.

Then he stopped playing, just as suddenly as he had started, and tried to make me remember the nightly games of Chinese checkers, our reward for dishes well done.

Odd person out would play the winner, jumping colored marbles over their opponent's, and my marbles were always blue. Winner of the winner had to clean up after the game.

"Look, Simon, it's a choice I make, not to remember. If I wanted to, I would."

He leaned back until his chair touched stucco, hands folded behind his head, staring up at the stars.

"Now why on earth," he said, "would you purposely choose not to remember the happiest year of your entire life?"

"Kind of hard to explain."

Which was a lie. I couldn't imagine anything easier to explain; in fact, I couldn't imagine why something so simple and obvious should even require explanation.

"If you can't explain it to me, Ella, then you couldn't very damn well explain it to anybody."

I sighed, leaned my head back and picked out the Little Dipper and Cassiopeia. "Because then every single day I'm alive I'd have to feel the lack of it."

He never answered, just played "The City of New Orleans," a little slower and more mournful than usual.

He stopped in mid-song and apologized for doing such a lousy job of bringing me up.

I had to consider that a minute before answering.

"I thought you did pretty okay, actually."

"But I was never there. After Mrs. Hurley's house, I was never there."

That was impossible to argue; in fact, I could have added that even when he was there he wasn't there, but of course I didn't. Still, it seemed on a par with me apologizing to Simon for growing up unstable. What else could we have been for each other? We were only dealt certain cards from which to form a hand.

"You did good for a kid," I said.

This talk brought up a kind of restlessness, an unfinished feeling, and I thought I needed to change the subject.

So I said, "Do you ever wish you'd been an astronomer instead, Simon?"

And he said, "Every single day I'm alive."

For the first time since my talk with Virgil, over fifteen years earlier, I felt lucky to have no dreams. Because I knew I'd feel the lack of them, every day I'm alive.

WALKING BACK ALONE

WE ARRIVE BACK at the cave to find coyotes. At least a dozen of them, gnawing the bones of last night's kill, the remains of my dinner. Their heads shoot up to watch us; Yozzy dances but I quiet her with a hand on her shoulder.

They stare out of narrow eyes, lick greasy flews. Their legs seem foolishly thin beneath their great ruffs of mane. They do not run away. They wait to decide.

I slide down from Yozzy's back, stand with the rifle butt against my thigh, flip off the safety and fire a round into the metallic sky of morning. I've decided for them. They run.

I reload immediately, pull a loose cartridge from my pocket, slam it into the chamber as a bold female circles around behind Yozzy and nips at her heels, as if testing. Will you kick, or allow yourself to be hamstrung?

Yozzy strikes out with her hooves, and the aggressor arcs and tries a second pass. I shoot a round aimed in her direction, but low. For a split second I think the kick of the rifle will raise the shot, and I will take her. It's not my intention, but I'll live with it.

Dirt explodes a foot in front of her, spraying into her face and eyes. She yelps as if shot, which she isn't, and runs to join her pack. They move fifty or so feet away, then sit watching.

I walk Yozzy onto the rock plateau outside the cave.

I spread out my sleeping bag for Yozzy, but she no longer seems interested in collapsing. I take that as a good sign. We are more rested now. She stands, as horses normally will, and I lie back on the bag, my back against the stone of the mesa, and watch the coyotes.

I think, *it's morning, you vampires. Fly away home.* I tilt my hat down against the rising sun.

In time I wake. I sit up and see Yozzy far away on the plain. I see the coyotes have given up and gone.

I fall asleep again with the rifle still resting across my knees. Night is the time to travel. Tonight we must give up and go home.

When the sun goes down, I decide to take the full water bottles along. Nothing is more important than water. Nothing will ever erase, or allow me to forget, watching Yozzy nearly die for the lack of it. We are no longer on a brave quest, with the entire universe supposedly lined up at our backs in support and awe. We are simply walking back.

Of course, I would not ask Yozzy to carry all that water and me. She has done enough already, sacrificed too much for too little. She stands below the rock ledge and I fold the blanket several times to form a pad, to protect her from the cloth strap that holds the necks of the two bottles together. Then I carefully settle the bottles across her withers.

We set off on foot.

We walk for most of the night. I follow Yozzy. I walk beside her, but I bend as she bends; I let her take us where she wants us to go. She is not heading straight back the way we came, as far as I can tell. She seems to be veering east, toward the wash. This is probably good thinking. The water on her back is nearly gone. A few gallons of water is nothing, if you are a horse. I wince with every step, take it anyway, and I project ten steps ahead. I know I'll never make it. A few miles down, I think. Probably three dozen to go. I can't keep track anymore. I need sleep.

An hour later I see the trees of the wash in the far distance, water, shade. I feel almost as though we might survive this journey; to have believed otherwise, in the first few miles, seemed a frightening omen.

The sun rises again as we walk toward that ribbon of green. It is farther away from us than I allowed myself to believe.

I stop and give Yozzy the last of the water, pouring it into my hat and offering it to her. I take only a swallow for myself. Now I believe it's fair to ask her to carry me again.

I use a rock to mount, and I hold the sleeping bag against my left thigh; the rifle droops against my right. The reins lie untouched across Yozzy's shoulders, and she navigates.

I feel a great relief, my feet dangling comfortably.

Heat rises in shimmery waves, disturbing the continuity of the landscape, and I begin to fear the green trees are only a tease, a mirage, but we do reach them, and they're real.

I slide down, pull off my shoes, and we stand in the cool water together, me in my wet socks, Yozzy on sore hooves; then I lie down and roll around, soaking my clothes.

I fill my hat, turn my face to the sky and pour water over my head.

I lean back on a tree trunk, in its scant but blessed shade. I have to sleep. We have to stay here, Yozzy standing with her feet in the cool water of the wash, already shallower than it was the night before. We can't walk now until sundown. I fear I cannot walk at all, yet I know we'll have to load up on water again, at some point, and I'll have to set out on foot. In the meantime I need to sleep. I can only avoid it for just so long. I sit with my knees drawn up, the rifle across them, watching Yozzy nibble and drink.

I wake because a voice tells me to. It's not my voice. It's not the voice of anyone I know. It's only words in my head.

Wake up.

The voice conveys such a sense of panic that I grab for the rifle across my knees, but it isn't there. I look at the ground, feel the ground all around me, but I didn't simply drop the rifle. It's gone. The sun beats into my eyes from directly overhead; I hope this is all part of a dream.

Then I see him. Lying on his belly in the wash, his beard in the cool water, his blanket cape moving slightly with the pull of the wash toward home. He has taken his rifle back, pressed his eye to the sight; he is aiming, ready to fire. But not at me.

I try to leap to my feet, but my hips have stiffened in sleep, I have painful sores on the insides of my thighs from riding, my feet have been bleeding again, and the dried blood has cemented my soles to my socks. But, out of necessity, I do make it to my feet.

I look up the wash in the direction his rifle is pointing, and I see Yozzy, grazing a few dozen yards upstream. He is aiming to shoot my horse.

I move without thinking. I move faster than any thinking process would allow. I must pitch forward through the air at some point because I could swear I land on his back before my feet touch the water. The rifle goes off, and in my peripheral vision I see Yozzy spook sideways and canter a few yards away.

I hook one arm under the wild man's throat, applying the kind of pressure that rage and fear evoke in someone who would not normally possess great physical strength. Suddenly I'm on my back in the wash, my advantage lost, waiting to die. Waiting for his hands around my throat, waiting for him to pick up the rifle and aim it at my face. But he doesn't pick up the rifle. He doesn't take advantage of my moment of helplessness.

He runs away.

I look to Yozzy, who is watching me with her neck straight, her head held high. In her moment of attention she looks younger and more beautiful. She is alive and, as far as I can see, unhit.

I pick the rifle up from a patch of tangled grass growing out of the water, wondering in a distant, disconnected way how wet it might be, whether it's safe to fire a wet rifle, knowing that I am about to learn my answer the hard way.

I stand with the shallow water flowing over my wet socks and aim the rifle at the retreating figure, the running man who killed my brother, who tried to kill my horse. I steady the rifle at my shoulder, squeeze my eye tightly against the scope. The crosshairs rest right between his shoulder blades. I squeeze off a shot.

For some reason the dry click surprises me. I'm not sure why it should. I know the rifle now, I've used it to save Yozzy from coyotes; I know it must be reloaded between shots. Yet somehow I expected the rifle to concuss against my shoulder, the metallic ringing to linger in my head, to hamper my hearing; I expected the wild man to fall.

I watch the running figure disappear over a distant rise.

I turn back to Yozzy and lower the rifle. She picks her way back to me. I examine her carefully, run my hands along her neck, across her sides, down her legs. As if she could be hurt and I wouldn't know, wouldn't see. As if I can't trust my eyes to tell me. She is unharmed. We are all unharmed.

And if I had shot the wild man? I think about that as I settle again under the tree, as I pull a wet cartridge from my pocket and reload, just in case. How would I have explained that to the world, to those whose job it is to inquire? He tried to kill my horse, so I shot him. In the back, at several hundred paces, as he was running away.

And yet part of me wishes I had. Part of me wishes the wild man had left me a double-barreled shotgun. One chance to make things right. But maybe I would have missed anyway. I'm not a cowboy. I'm not a crack shot. So far I've only practiced on coyotes. I'm not sure if I could shoot a man at this distance with only a rifle and the sheer will to do so.

We wait out the day's heat in this place, but of course I no longer enjoy the luxury of sleep.

THEN:

HERE'S SOMETHING I remember about Simon. Almost a real something, in retrospect.

I was four years old, DeeDee six, Simon ten, about to become the man of the family.

Our mother used to read to us at bedtime. She'd sit at the edge of DeeDee's bed; Simon would come in from his room, in his robe and slippers, and sit on the end of mine. On the night in question, she read another installment of our ongoing trip through *The Wind in the Willows.*

She and my father had been fighting. We could hear him scream at her, as we brushed our teeth, as we changed into our pajamas, systematically avoiding each other's eyes.

When she came in to read, at the usual time, her eyes looked puffy and red, her breathing sounded uneven, but she offered a forced smile and began that night's chapter, and we all fell silently into our family pact. Why is this night no different from all other nights?

There is a line from *The Wind in the Willows* that burned itself on me like a mental tattoo: "Up popped Ratty."

As my mother read this, we heard my father's car start in the driveway. She threw the book on the floor.

"No," she said, in a hushed tone, as if we wouldn't hear, wouldn't notice. She ran to the window, threw it open, screamed his name out into the night. "Gabe!"

Looking out from my post in bed, looking past her out the window, I saw lights switch on in neighboring houses.

Our mother ran out of the room. Simon picked up the book, and sat in her spot, on the end of DeeDee's bed.

"Up popped Ratty," he said, as if we'd all enjoyed the line so much the first time, we might care to hear it again. I suppose he was only being a letter-perfect reader, assuring himself that we all remembered just where we had left off. Behind and underneath his voice, we heard them shout at each other in the driveway, heard the squeal of tires, our mother's curses, in a volume to follow him through the night.

Simon finished reading us the book over the next twelve nights. Our mother never read to us again.

With that one simple stroke, Simon appointed himself torchbearer, seeing to it that every story had an ending.

Trouble is, I never heard another word of *The Wind in the Willows*. The last words I can remember are *up popped Ratty*.

DARK FOREST

WE RIDE AWAY into dusk. If we ride all night, maybe we could make it to Sam Roanhorse's by daybreak. Or could we? What has it cost us to travel along the wash? I am guessing it runs east, farther away from Everett's all the time, or he would have suggested it. How many miles have we sacrificed? Five or six at the top of our journey—how many more when we cut west again? Has the thirty-mile walk to Sam's house become fifty?

And when we turn from the wash, water bottles full, will I be able to walk that far, or at all?

We ride through blackness, under a dome of stars. The empty plastic bottles bump against my knees.

The stars are all around us. I wonder if they would remind Simon of anything, if Simon were here.

We make a final stop at the wash. Yozzy drinks. I slide down and open my sleeping bag, and pack all my belongings at the bottom—which I had not thought of earlier—and throw it double across her back to cushion her against the weight of full bottles. I suggest we stop to rest, but she does not stop. We turn west and walk.

Before I hoist the bottles onto her back again, I apologize to her. For the difficulty of the journey, all hers. For the danger. For the miles. For the load.

Nonsense, she says. *We came here to do just this, and we are doing it.*

We walk off into the night, away from the wash. Away from our best shot at survival. I don't know where Sam's house is, I don't know where I am, but I trust Yozzy, even as a part of me tightens, worries for our future.

The moon glows yellow over the horizon, casting shadows of rock formations and stands of scrub, like ghosts or demons, like the netherworlds and dark forests of the fantasy tale that is my real life. I know now I fear this land.

When sunrise comes at last, we are nowhere. We are not near anything. We have no shade. I hope Yozzy knows where we are. We bake in the sun all day. I open out the sleeping bag, drape it over parts of us for shade, but it is never enough. When night comes we are out of water. So at least I can ride.

I ride through blackness, under stars, beyond hunger pangs, beyond exhaustion, but dizzy from fasting, from lack of sleep. Yozzy lays her ears back now and then, and I whip my head around to see what she hears. To see if he is back there, stalking us. Once I think I see a moonshadow move in the dark, but it could have been the sudden motion of my eyes. It could have been an illusion or an animal.

I remind myself that he is unarmed, as far as I know.

I tie my shirttail through the trigger guard of the rifle, lean onto Yozzy's neck and surrender to sleep.

I wake up on the ground. I have landed on the rifle, its barrel bruising my ribs. I jump up to see Yozzy on her knees, struggling to rise. I wait with her until she finds her feet again. I do not try to mount.

We walk side by side, and I shiver with a deep cold, running into the center of my sleepiest place, but the walking brings my temperature up. I feel the cold but don't mind it so much.

I walk until my feet beg not to touch the ground, but I force them to. I try to make myself lighter, but the lightest step brings pain. I walk until I can't walk, but I can't stop, and there's no carpet of madness, nowhere to sweep the pain; it's mine, I have only to live with it.

I walk until I see a house, just a dot on the horizon, with a thin trail of smoke, suggesting life. I walk until I know I can't walk to this house. I walk until Yozzy goes down again, striking her knees on the hard, unforgiving ground.

She throws her weight forward as if to rise, sinks to her knees again. I wait. She tries again, and this time finds her feet.

Her left knee bleeds a little, and I tear a long strip of my shirt-tail, and tie it around, not too tightly, mostly so she won't grind dirt into it when she falls again.

I hold her with my arms around her neck, and I talk into her warm coat, but I don't know what I say, or if it is important.

We set off, the two of us, on foot, side by side toward the house I pray is Sam's. Failing that, any house will do.

I walk with my unrolled sleeping bag around my shoulders for warmth.

I walk until I would rather die than walk. I feel my palm on the cool barrel of the killer's rifle, and I know what I would do if I was out here alone. I would hold the barrel in my mouth, like some thin, wordless Hemingway, and write my own ending to all this pain.

But I am not out here alone. I will not give up with Yozzy watching, or rather, watching myself through her eyes.

I walk some more.

In time I fall to my knees, like Yozzy intermittently does, and I cannot get up. I sit for a moment, and she waits for me, stares silently, blinks and waits.

When I'm ready to move on, I rise only to my knees. I will crawl to Sam's house. I watch it grow large in the distance, and I am more convinced that it is Sam's house. After all, Yozzy leads me to it. Doesn't that say enough?

I crawl until my knees ache, and the heels of my hands are raw, and I straighten onto my knees, upright, and try to breathe, and try not to breathe, but I have to. It's my job.

Such a short distance left to go, my eyes say. As I kneel in the dirt, watching Sam's house in the distance, Yozzy lowers her great weight gently, to curl by my side.

I don't know how long we stay that way. I don't know how or even if we cover that last mile.

I just remember us, looking off in the direction of Sam Roanhorse's house together, watching another day break to the east.

THEN:

WHEN I WAS a baby, my brother Simon used to pick me up and hold me. Whether he thought I'd serve as a teddy bear, or whether he knew I would soon need one, I don't know.

I know I'm not supposed to remember back so far. I've grown tired of being told that no such thing is possible, and as a result, I rarely admit early memories out loud.

In fact, I remember being born with the caul, and by this I don't mean that I remember hearing about it. I remember the caul, and then the sudden absence of it.

DeeDee stared into my crib when I was a baby, as though weighing me with her eyes. I knew, in some wordless way, that I was destined to love her more than she loved me. These lines are drawn early, and we only pretend we'll cross or transcend them. Or so I believe.

Simon held on.

I cried if he handed me back to my mother. My mother, I sensed, held me through some prearranged debt of duty, one she might retract, if such a thing were possible. When she grew tired of the squalling, she'd hand me back to Simon.

Simon could have hated me, this baby girl born to steal his attention in the midst of his crisis of supply. But he chose to hold on.

When the caul was removed, which I realize I am not supposed to remember, I felt my first pain. In my eyes, and my head, from the searing brightness of a world I'd never invited.

I thought it was my last defense, my last covering.

But there would be others.

And then, later, there wouldn't be.

FUNERALS FOR HORSES

ON SAM ROANHORSE'S couch, I wake from a long sleep, my feet bare and swollen, a thin wool blanket thrown over me, which I push away.

Sam sits at his table, watching.

"Don't you have to open the store?" I say.

"I open the store when I please. It's not like there's another gun shop just down the road. Besides," he says, "it's Sunday."

I'm stunned by the revelation. Imagine, the days of the week continuing in order while we were away. As if nothing at all had happened, or changed.

Then, as if plucked late from a dream, I say, "I didn't find my brother. I don't think there is a Simon anymore."

Sam smiles. "Then good thing for you that there is an Ella."

I rest, and eat, and drink water, and adjust to this Simonless world in the peace of Sam Roanhorse's home. The following morning I hobble out to Sam's truck, and Sam says Yozzy will rest, and eat, and drink water, and in a day or two she will find her way home. She knows the way.

I ask to say goodbye to her, and Sam leads her to the passenger side of the truck, with a brown hand on her jaw, and she pushes her face through the open window and I thank her. I tell her we'll see each other in just a matter of days. I do not say any of this out loud. She offers no reaction to this at all, as though she hasn't decided, or won't share her decision at this time, just puffs warm breath into my face, and I lay my cheek against her jaw, then kiss the soft pink skin of her upper lip.

As Sam starts the truck's engine, she picks her way back to the shade. She hurts. I feel it.

We ride in a comforting silence to Everett's house; May smiles widely to see us. Everett is gone. Driven to the city to try to help his son, who is in trouble again.

The diner looks clean, nearly ready to open. Usable. Though I know it won't open until the season brings change. Cars. I can't imagine so much was done in just a handful of days, or that it has only been that long, and that the world went on without us, not knowing.

May dishes up a steaming bowl of mutton stew.

"How was your trip?" she asks. "Did you find what you were looking for?"

"I didn't find what I thought I was looking for," I say. "But I found something I didn't know was missing."

"Even better," she says. "Eat now."

I sleep well, in my sleeping bag under the stars, and I stay three days, during which Yozzy does not come back.

On the third night I have a bad dream. I dream I'm sitting atop the wild man, the killer, with my knife to his throat. And he speaks to me in plain English, his voice startlingly familiar.

He says, "I'm sorry, Ella."

I drop the knife and sit down hard beside him. He doesn't reach for it. He rolls onto his belly and cries into his hands, and for a minute or two I just watch him, unable to answer any questions of myself, or to ask any.

I take hold of his blanket, and pull hard, until he turns to face me, and I hold a handful of his soft, tangled white hair, as if in anger, though I feel none.

I look at his red, strained eyes again. "Simon?" He doesn't say yes or no, but the renewal of his tears reveals the place I've touched in him. "How could you be? How could you be Simon? You don't even look like him."

But I keep looking, as I tell him these things, and the goosebumps wash through me again, and, like the stroke of an ax, his eyes break through to the center.

I have seen Simon's eyes.

"My god, Simon, do you know what I've gone through to find you?"

But his eyes, which are the eyes of the wild man again, know nothing of me, or of my struggles. Nor do they care.

I open my eyes and see the stars above the Ankeah home, and I lie on my back under them, and I don't go back to sleep, nor do I want to. For a moment I hear a rustling in the brush and I jump to my feet and call for Yozzy, but it's only some small animal burrowing into cover.

The light is on in the Ankeah kitchen. I knock softly, and May calls me in. She's at the wooden table, drinking a cup of tea. She motions for me to sit with her.

"I had a bad dream," I say. Just for this moment my voice sounds like the voice of a child. All children have bad dreams. When I had them, I used to run to Simon.

May gets up to put the kettle back on. She seems plumper in her nightshirt, and she looks sad. "I had one, too," she says.

My stomach goes cold, and I think it's going to happen again. One of those dreams that get around. "About a wild man?"

She shakes her head and squeezes out one sad little smile. "About my son."

"Oh. Sorry. I thought maybe our dream was the same."

"Maybe our hurt is the same," she says, and comes back to sit with me. "What did you dream?"

"I saw that man. The man I thought killed Simon. But he was Simon. I knew that, May. I knew it at the time. I wouldn't let myself know it."

"Well," she says, "you just saw that he was not your brother. But now you can see that he is the man who used to be."

"I tried to shoot him, May. I tried to kill my own brother. I told myself I was shooting at Simon's killer. But part of me knew."

The kettle sings. May gets up to make me a cup of tea. She pours the boiling water through a strainer into my cup. She doesn't speak for a time, and I'm glad. I don't want her to rush to absolve me. I only want whatever absolution she is genuinely able to locate, whatever truly belongs to me.

She sits across the table, looks into my face, slides the cup over to me, and the warm steam rises to meet me. "You shot at the man who took your brother Simon away from you."

"What happened to him, May?"

"Since he was your brother, probably much the same thing that happened to you. He probably tried for too long to pretend it didn't happen."

I take a long, hot sip of tea. "I always thought you were the one who didn't say much."

She smiles, a little underdone smile. "Depends on what there is to say. You can't save him."

"He saved me."

"Then you must have wanted him to."

Now she has hit at the center of my disappointment. Simon saw me. He must have known it was me. He must have known I'd come all that way to save him.

He must not have wanted me to.

Headlights sweep across the kitchen and May's eyes come up. Her head tilts slightly, reading the sound of the motor. "Everett is home," she says.

We sit quietly for a minute, and the engine cuts off, the truck door slams, and Everett joins us in the kitchen. His mood feels heavy to me, dark, more than I wish to carry. And I am feeling things acutely now, as if my nerves were all exposed. I think this is what it feels like to be sane.

"May," he says. "Ella."

"Are you hungry?" May asks him.

He shakes his head. He sets one big hand on my shoulder. "Were you able to find your brother?"

"Yes and no. Were you able to help your son?"

"Yes and no. I'm going to get some sleep."

When he has left the room May shakes her head, as if to clear the sadness away. "He's never been anything but trouble."

"Everett?"

"Our son."

"Oh. Of course."

"Everett thinks we raised him all wrong. But do you know anybody who raised their kids all right?"

"Not personally, no. May, why hasn't Yozzy come back?"

She shakes her head. I'm not sure why I thought she would know.

In the morning Everett and I load into the pickup and drive to Sam Roanhorse's.

Sam says Yozzy left for home almost two days ago, and my heart falls, and it's held up so high, by such narrow lashings, I wonder how far it has to drop, and what will become of it now.

We ride the open countryside, off the road, toward home, and I kneel in the truck bed, my hands flat against the roof of the cab. I ask for guidance on where to look.

When I see her, I knock on Everett's window and point.

We drive up close to her, and she lifts her head. She's spread out on her side. She does not try to get up. I limp, hobble to her, and Everett follows close behind.

I hold her neck, and whisper to her, but her eyes are hollow, filmy, and she says only, *thank you for coming,* and *goodbye.*

"The trip was too much for her," I say.

Everett says, "No, it was exactly enough. She's done what you needed. She's done."

A minute later he's back at my side carrying Simon's rifle. I'm shocked to see it. I had no idea he'd brought it, but now, in a deep place, moving deeper all the time, like quicksand, I understand.

"You or me?" he asks.

"It should be her owner," I say, in a voice that might not belong to me.

He hands me the rifle. I don't ask why. I wait for him to explain.

"She has no owner. She belongs to herself. You gave her what I never could. You gave her something important to do."

He leaves us alone.

I cry into her neck, and remember the pain of my own walking, and the coyotes who tried to take her, and how they'll never have her now.

"Yozzy," I say. "I think we found Simon after all. I don't think we can help him, but I think we found him. I just wanted you to know that. Thank you. Goodbye now."

I need her to know this before she goes, though I suspect I am the only one who needed to hear it again.

Her eyes say she understands this moment, and my role in it, and that she's more than ready. I kiss her on the nose, and rise to my knees, and set the rifle to point into her ear.

I remember this from the deer on the Sacramento highway.

When I feel I've set the rifle properly, I remind her that I love her and I look to the sky, not down. I ask my finger to do the unthinkable, and it must be wiser than the rest of me, because it does.

I hear, but I never see.

I keep my eyes closed, and as her soul leaves, a part of me leaves to follow, a horse part, something I loved dearly but no longer need.

I turn away without looking, limp back to the truck, and ask Everett to please check to see that I've done the job correctly.

When he returns he puts a hand on my shoulder and says, "Perfect."

"What do you do with a dead horse in the Navajo tradition?" He only shrugs.

I thought there was a tradition for everything, every passage, but Everett says the traditions are ancient, from a time when there were no horses in America. He suggests we leave her where she is. He says even if we had a way to do so it's a crime to bury a thousand pounds of food, sustenance, that the native animals could use.

"I don't want the coyotes to have her."

"They can't, Ella, she's gone. It's just her body."

"But I worked so hard to protect her."

"Of course you did. You needed her. She needed herself. Let that change now."

We drive home in silence.

Halfway home I see him up ahead of us, hobbling along by the side of the highway, moving in the same direction we are. He is wearing the overalls, one strap on his right shoulder holding the baggy things in place, the bib drooping on the left where I cut a strap away. For whatever reason, I assume that what I am seeing is not real.

"Everett, do you have mirages around here?"

"That man, you mean? Is that your brother Simon?"

"No. But I think he used to be."

We pull up close, close enough to see his white hair flapping out behind him in the hot breeze. Everett slows the truck as we pull alongside him.

"Don't stop," I say. I'm thinking of Yozzy, thinking that this wild former Simon tried to shoot her. "He's not my brother anymore."

Everett crawls the truck along, a mile or two an hour, beside the man, who does not turn to look. "But if he used to be, maybe he could be again."

I roll my window all the way down. "Simon," I say. He is not more than three feet from me. I could lean out and touch him, but I don't. He turns his head slightly at the sound of his name. "Simon, where are you going?"

"Going home, Ella."

"Good. That's a good thing to do, Simon." I wish he would turn and look at me. I want to see it in his eyes, the way I did in my dream. I know for certain now, because he called me by my name. But I want to see Simon in him. It doesn't make sense inside me, how much he has changed. "Sarah misses you."

"How is Sarah?" he says, and the voice is close to something now, riding on the edge of a voice I know.

"Worried sick about you."

"I'll go home, tell her I'm okay."

"Good. That's good, Simon."

He continues to shuffle along the road beside us. He shifts his eyes over to look at me, indirectly, assessing in his periphery. I assume I am the source of his interest, but I've forgotten that I have his rifle between my knees, pointed straight up to the roof of the truck cab, both hands steady on the barrel.

"That's mine, you know," he says. Childlike and resentful.

"Yes, it is. You won't need it in Sacramento, though. I thought maybe we'd leave it here with my friend Everett. Would that be okay?"

"I guess."

"I have your wallet. Maybe you want it back now."

He stops walking. Everett brakes a few feet beyond him, then shifts the truck into reverse and backs even with Simon in the middle of the road, which is otherwise empty. No car in sight in either direction.

I say, "Look at me, Simon," and he does. And it's Simon. "I'm going home, too, Simon. Maybe we could travel together. It would be almost like old times."

He seems to think about this for a few moments. He looks down at the dirt under his bare feet. Up at the sky. Then he nods his head and climbs onto the truck bed, and we all head back to the Ankeahs'.

After lunch Simon bathes, and I borrow a pair of scissors from May, and ask Simon's permission to groom him. He nods, wide-eyed, and asks how short his hair will be, and if I'll leave a mustache.

"A mustache? Oh, yes, I think we should. Don't you? As far as the hair goes, it's going to go pretty short, because it's so tangled. But it'll grow fast."

I cut just below each matted knot—through the center of some—and brush out what's left. He doesn't fuss, though I'm sure it pulls. When I can comb through it, I even it out as best I can.

I trim his beard close to the skin, then lather his face with soap and shave him with a borrowed razor. He holds still, seeming to almost enjoy the attention. I make faces at him, to suggest how I'd like him to hold his mouth, to help me shave more closely.

I towel away the last soap, and he looks almost like Simon again. The eyes have changed, he's too thin, but the mouth and mustache look familiar; the hair is blonde again, because it was never white. The surface was only bleached by the sun.

He says, "I want to go home now."

"What made you change your mind?"

"Because you came all this way to find me. How did you find me, Ella?"

"I'm not sure. I just tried to think like somebody who knows you. Why did you try to shoot my horse?"

"So you wouldn't ride away again. Thanks for coming for me, Ella."

The blanket May gave him to wear has fallen off one shoulder, and I see the angry scars of sunburn blisters, deep and maybe permanent, and I want to touch them, as if my touch could heal somehow. I want to know how someone could allow such a thing to happen. Before I do, I see the scars on my own wrist, as I reach out, and the overlay of the two brings a sense of quiet, of no questions, in my mind. I ask too many questions anyway.

"How do I look?" he says.

I ask May for a mirror, and she gives me a small hand-held one, and smiles at Simon, and runs a hand over his short, clean hair. I hold the mirror for him, and he sees himself. His face changes, from surprise to embarrassment to something I can't read, or don't dare.

"Kind of short."

"I know. I'm sorry. It'll grow fast. When we get to the next town, I'll buy you a hat."

"Really?"

"Well, it's your money, actually."

I turn the mirror around and look at myself. My hair is tangled, my face clean, red, windburned, the scar on my chin still visible. My eyes are the same, only better. I sigh in relief.

"What do you see, Ella?"

"Just me, Simon. Only me."

Everett comes in and shakes Simon's hand, and he likes Simon, and Simon likes him. I don't have to ask this, I know. But then, I think, everybody likes my brother Simon. Everybody always has.

We sit out on the porch, and Everett smokes, and I keep my feet propped up, and the cool air of evening washes over us like a river, washes us away, but not too far, and we are as close to home as we will come on our way home.

I hear Everett tell Simon that the man he was is not gone, only joined by other men he was, but knew nothing about.

I leave them there to talk.

In time Everett brings a pile of wood out to the yard and sets it beside me, where I sit staring north, toward Sam's house, and beyond. He builds a fire with three or four sticks, then throws on another two when it's burning well.

"What's that for?" I ask.

"Keep it burning for three days. It's a funeral offering. It will help you mourn."

"I thought there was no tradition."

"Well, you needed one, so I made one up."

I sit cross-legged in front of the fire until sundown, defying the stiffness in my legs. I feed it wood if it appears weak. I watch the cold northern landscape through its waves of heat. I watch the sparks and smoke and ash rise, always rise, with the heat, like the things we discard, whether they were part or all of what we thought we were.

The moon, which is also rising, smiles across this moment.

My brother Simon comes to sit with me at dark, brings me dinner, and I thank him and set it aside. He sits in silence with me for a long portion of night, and rises from time to time to feed another stick of wood into the flames.

I lie down and stare at the stars, because the heat hurts my eyes. The stars are always cool. The stars never change. Or, if they do, within our lifetime the change is unnoticeable.

Simon speaks up in the stillness.

He says, "I'm sorry I tried to shoot her."

"I'm sorry I tried to shoot you."

"You did? Oh. Well, anyway. You missed."

"I'm not cut out for this stuff." I sit up, close beside him, and loop my arm around his shoulder, and kiss him on the temple, and lean my head against his. "What happened, Simon? When did everything fall apart for you?"

He seems to know the answer sooner than he shares it. "All along, Ella. I guess nobody noticed."

I look to the moon, hanging three-quarters full over the horizon. It says, *see what I told you? Things have been shifting all this time.*

"Why did you leave your checkbook in your coat pocket, Simon? Did you want me to find you?"

He considers this for a long time.

"Checkbook?" he repeats. He seems confused, and I realize he has no memory of owning a checkbook at all. I nod at the moon, nod my understanding.

He begins to speak again, then catches himself.

"What?"

"Oh, you get mad when I talk about Mrs. Hurley."

"Maybe I've gotten better at it in my old age."

He sighs, like he isn't sure enough to try, and it reminds me so much of twelve-year-old Simon, it gives me goosebumps. "You know the last thing she said to me before she died?" I expect a rehash of just what she said to me. *Take care of that sister of yours.* Pretty much negating the value of the whole deal, turning it into a weak admonition not to turn on each other. "She said if I ever needed someone to lean on I should remember my sister Ella. She said you're a lot stronger than you look."

I laugh, and say it's not the first time she was ever wrong.

"She wasn't wrong. She was never wrong."

She was wrong, sometimes. But not about this. She knew I would turn out strong. She knew Simon would break under the strain. She noticed, and she tried to tell me. But I don't try to say all that to Simon.

"Well, she wasn't perfect, Simon. By her own admission. Remember what she used to say? 'I have two major flaws, both in my own eyes, and the eyes of the Lord. A taste for strong spirits and a feel for games of chance. But I go to church every Sunday, and if the good Lord took exception, he's had ample chance to mention it by now.'" I even get the voice down fairly well. Simon stares, wide-eyed, and for a minute I think I've angered him. Then I see he's amazed and impressed.

"You really do remember."

"Yes, I really do."

He leans back and closes his eyes. "She was right in the long run. When will we go home, Ella?"

"When the fire goes out. Then we'll be all done here. Then we'll go."

He falls asleep beside me, and I stroke the slight remainder of his hair. I build up the fire before I go to sleep.

THE END